A USA TODAY BESTSELLING BOOK

Book One in The JACK REACHER Cases

THE RIGHT MAN FOR REVENGE

Set in the Reacher universe by permission of Lee Child

DAN AMES

Copyright © 2017 by Dan Ames

Published by Slogan Books, Inc., New York, NY.

FREE BOOKS AND MORE

Would you like a FREE copy of my story BULLET RIVER?

To sign up for the DAN AMES BOOK CLUB, go to AuthorDanAmes.com

THE RIGHT MAN FOR REVENGE

The Jack Reacher Cases

Set in the REACHER universe.
By permission of Lee Child.

By

Dan Ames

"The more laws, the less justice."
-Cicero

CHAPTER ONE

The big man didn't hear the sound of the rifle being fired. He didn't have a sense that a bullet was hurtling toward him at thousands of feet per second. For him, it was a day like any other.

On the road, moving from one town to the next.

A vague destination in mind, maybe a cup of coffee and breakfast in a local diner, the soundtrack provided by the locals discussing politics or the high school sports team's victory or loss with the appropriate level of enthusiasm.

As the bullet bore down on him, the big man's mind reverted to the road ahead of him.

How different it was than the typical highway he was used to traversing. Instead of long, straight patches of sunbaked asphalt, this was a mountain road in the Pacific Northwest, well saturated with frequent rain. Towering evergreens flanked both sides of the road and prevented the sun from heating and drying the pavement.

The big man was running calculations in his mind, a comparison between distance traveled when elevation was a factor. It wasn't as easy as walking a long, flat stretch, but the big man was in excellent shape.

He shrugged his massive shoulders. He was at least 6'5" with a deep chest and narrow waist. Lean. Tough. He had on blue jeans. A shirt with a toothbrush in the pocket. Both looked like they were brand-new. His shoes were English.

His last thought was a statistical analysis of what the view ahead would look like when he topped the rise and the road curved back down toward a valley, most likely.

When the bullet hit the back of his head, it blew it apart with a velocity that drove his upper body forward.

The sound of the shot startled a trio of ravens who flocked to the sky.

The man folded at the waist and toppled forward. He landed on the side of the road amid hard-packed gravel and a few hardy weeds.

While his immense body was intact, most of his head was gone. Blood gushed from the stem of his neck, pooled, and ran down the slope of the embankment.

No human being heard the sound of the rifle, except for the shooter, who looked down from above at what was left of the target. Satisfied, the killer stood, retrieved the shell casing, and placed the rifle back in its case.

While the lonely road saw little traffic, eventually someone would see the body. The shooter planned to be well down the road before that happened.

Down on the embankment, the last of the big man's blood had finished spilling from his body.

Nothing moved and nothing happened until the next morning, when a car carrying a pair of hikers driving toward the trailhead slowed at the sight of a small group of turkey vultures gathered around the remains of a human being.

The hikers called the authorities and when the police

arrived, they summoned a crime scene team and notified dispatch that initial observations pointed toward a homicide.

First responders instantly surmised the likelihood of a gunshot to the back of the victim's head, resulting in chunks of the man's unrecognizable face decorating the ground a few feet from the body.

At least, the pieces that hadn't been snatched up by the hungry birds.

The crime scene technicians were fast but thorough, and one of them soon managed to extract the contents of the dead man's pocket, which consisted of two items.

A toothbrush.

And an ATM card.

A slight rain had begun to fall, and it began to wash away some of the blood splatter covering the dirt and gravel.

The crime tech used a flashlight to read the name on the ATM card.

JACK REACHER.

CHAPTER TWO

The first time he felt the joy of killing, Archibald Sica was just eight years old. He was working on his uncle's farm an hour southeast of Guadalajara.

There was a well, with several long pieces of wood placed into the vertical shaft. The bottoms of the wood planks were buried in water. The tops of the planks were at the mouth of the well, which itself was raised and fashioned into a square out of cement. It was like a viewing area into the depth of the well.

It wasn't a deep well, just ten feet or so. The planks were twelve feet long, enabling a person to stand at the top of the well and use the plank to stir the bottom, or help retrieve something if it fell into the well.

And at the bottom of the well there was only a few feet of water. It was mostly used to collect rainwater.

And lizards.

In that part of the country, there were plenty of lizards. And they liked to sunbathe about halfway up the wood planks. When they got too hot, they would slide off, dip into the water, and then climb back out.

Sica's uncle enjoyed the lizards, and had insisted the planks be left in the well to allow the lizards easy travel up and down the well.

At eight years old, Sica was just a boy, and had a young boy's stamina for work. Which meant he took frequent breaks when he could manage to sneak away.

As he was doing now.

The boy was hot, sweaty and tired. They were in the midst of harvesting crops and his job was to tie bundles of marijuana and load them onto the back of a pickup truck. He couldn't stop sneezing and his eyes were bleary. Plus, his arms were itchy.

He was hungry.

And a little bit angry at having to do so much work.

So when he leaned over the edge of the well, his forearms on the cement ledge, he studied the lizards. Some were bigger than others. Mostly green. A couple of them were a dark, mottled brown. There were slightly different tails. Some were long and straight, others were more upright, with a bit of a curl.

They stared ahead, surviving the heat just like everyone else.

Sica grabbed one of the planks and twisted it, then laughed as the lizards fell off into the water.

He was about to do the same to the others when he had an idea. He lifted the wood plank, which was very heavy for a boy his size, and raised the end from the water. He moved it over until its edge was directly above one of the fatter lizards with a curved tail.

And then Sica drove the plank downward.

The edge of the plank severed the lizard neatly in half. Blood squirted out onto the wood plank and the two halves of the lizard fell into the water.

Sica laughed.

Suddenly, he wasn't tired anymore.

He felt energized.

Happy.

He eyed the other lizards, nearly a half dozen on one of the other planks. He shuffled sideways, maintaining his grip on the plank. He raised it again and chopped downward six times, killing all of the lizards one after the other. They were either too tired, too lazy or too stupid to get out of the way. The boy marveled at how they could be so oblivious to their neighbors being slaughtered.

Where was their survival instinct?

Sica laughed again.

He repeated the action until every lizard in the well was chopped or smashed to death. The water had turned red, and chunks of lizard flesh floated to the surface.

The smell attracted flies who began to arrive at the top of the well.

Suddenly, the thrill of killing subsided for the boy and he realized what he had done. He dropped the plank and ran back to the field.

Later, word reached his uncle that the boy had murdered all of his pet lizards and Sica received a vicious beating.

But later, he thought it was worth it. The power. The pure joy of killing. Many years later he realized that scene at the well was a pivotal moment in his life. It helped him realize who he really was.

Now, some twenty-five years later, as he stared across the room at the terrified young man, Sica thought again of the primal joy he'd experienced at the well.

He glanced over at the center of the basement room and the deep square hole cut in the middle of the floor. It, too, was about ten feet deep. But it was much wider to accommodate Sica's exotic pets.

Like his uncle, the young boy had developed a fondness for reptiles.

Specifically, alligators.

Now, he nodded his head and two of his lieutenants carried the boy by his arms to the edge of the opening. He cried and tried to scream, but the duct tape across his mouth held steady. His feet churned in the air. His body thrashed but he wasn't strong enough to break the grips of the much bigger men.

The boy was a thief.

And now, he would be an example.

Two other men brought the young woman to the edge of the opening. Her hands were bound, and her feet were hobbled together with two sets of handcuffs.

She tried to look away, but one of the men grabbed her by the jaw and twisted her face until she had to watch the boy in front of her.

Sica raised his hand and dragged an invisible blade across his own throat.

One of his men cut the throat of the boy and threw his body into the opening.

There was a splash, and then moments later, thrashing.

Sica listened, as did the other young men assembled for the viewing. They were part of the thief's crew.

The young woman vomited onto the floor and the men returned her to her seat against the concrete wall.

Tears streamed down her face and her chest heaved.

Sica wanted everyone in the room to learn from the display.

His hope was that the young woman would understand just how much trouble she was in.

And he wanted his crew to understand they had a choice.

They could be loyal.

Or they could be food.

CHAPTER THREE

Former FBI Agent Lauren Pauling held the gun steady.

She aimed for the heart.

But just for fun, she tilted the muzzle up and fired five rounds straight through the head. Without hesitation. And with deadly accuracy.

"Come on, Lauren," the voice next to her said.

Pauling took off her ear protection gear and thumbed the button to bring the paper target back to her.

It was a great grouping.

Five rounds neatly stitched into the forehead of the gun range's paper target bad guy.

Part of the requirement to hold a private investigator's license in New York was to stay up to date with firearms training and requirements. Pauling loved to shoot. She spent frequent afternoons at the same indoor gun range just up the street from her apartment, and today, she'd invited a friend of hers, also a former agent, to the range.

Her friend's name was Haley Roberts and she now worked Internal Affairs for the NYPD.

"Head shots are for long distance," Haley said. "What were you trying to do, go all Hollywood on me?"

"I know," Pauling answered. "Sometimes, head shots are good therapy, though."

She ejected her spent shells and put the gun back into her case, which she slipped into her purse.

Roberts did the same and the two friends left the range.

They stepped out onto the busy street, where the sound of gunfire wouldn't be met with the same kind of casual indifference found at the gun range. At least, Pauling hoped not.

"Wine at my place?" Pauling asked.

"Nah, can't tonight," Roberts said. "Big meeting tomorrow with the chief about that thing."

Roberts was a tall black woman with an overbite and an athlete's body. Being a female and working Internal Affairs meant her popularity on the job was never very high.

But she was tough and strong. More importantly, she believed in what she was doing. Pauling admired her.

'That thing' was a department-wide bribe scandal that Roberts had managed to nip in the bud before it got out. Now, Pauling's friend was in charge of damage control and containment.

It was a big job and her friend was under a lot of pressure.

"Okay. Text me if you need any help," Pauling said as they parted.

It was a cool, late summer evening in New York and Pauling enjoyed the walk back to her apartment. The first touches of cold weather were just beginning to appear, and she made a mental note to take a look at her cold-weather wardrobe.

She made it back to her co-op near West 4th. The building was a renovated factory so her walls and ceiling were made of brick, at least two-feet thick. She opened her door and stepped inside. The apartment was light, bright and inviting. Even the smell, a vague sense of lavender, welcomed visitors.

Pauling set her keys on the kitchen counter and stowed her gear in her bedroom closet before washing her hands and returning to the kitchen for a glass of wine.

She had leftover grilled salmon in the fridge but she wasn't terribly hungry. The living room was cozy with muted rugs, soft textures and dark woods. Pauling sank into a brown leather chair and debated about turning on the television, or filling the space with some soft jazz and just relaxing.

She ended up doing neither because her cell phone rang.

She fished it from her front pocket and looked at the number.

It wasn't one she recognized.

"Hello?" she said.

The voice on the other end was scratchy and gender-neutral.

It spoke in an even, measured cadence.

"Jack Reacher is dead."

CHAPTER FOUR

The shooter climbed higher along the face of the mountain. It was cold and a steady wind tore at the killer's pale face. Loose stones tumbled down the side of the hill and a hawk flew far overhead, hunting a field mouse.

With an easy confidence, the shooter made good time. Every step seemed to have a little extra bounce to it.

The shot had been a good one.

It occurred to the killer that not many people could have pulled it off. This thought process didn't stem from arrogance. Or a conceited ego.

It came from professionalism.

A cold knowledge that, like a machine, the mechanics behind another killing had meshed with robotic precision. Perfectly calibrated to factor in the wind. The drop in elevation. It hadn't been easy.

Back in the day, the shooter would have had a spotter who'd worked out a lot of the calculations.

Those days were long gone, though.

The sniper worked alone. And it was better that way. It

was never good to depend on people, that's how mistakes were made. And in this business, the shooter knew, your first mistake was often your last.

The mountain leveled off and opened up into a deep meadow, filled with huge slabs of rock, long grass and a creek that ran through its middle. There were bear here, the shooter knew, and they tended not to like company.

There was no need to hurry. The body may or may not have been found yet, but that was now far away.

In this line of business it paid to train for endurance. Sometimes, like this one, the ability to exert oneself for extended periods of time was essential. But being in command physically was important for other reasons. A steady hand. Clarity of thought. The courage to kill.

The shooter continued on, weaving through a dim trail that ran roughly to the main path nearly a quarter mile away. No trace was left behind.

That was certainty.

They could study bullet trajectory, try to pinpoint the shooter's location and search for forensic evidence.

But they would find none.

Oh, they would probably be able to figure out the location, maybe even point to some slight disturbances in the dirt or grass, but it wouldn't tell them any kind of story. Wouldn't give them the narrative they were looking for.

They weren't dealing with an amateur here.

Quite the opposite.

This wasn't the shooter's first mission.

That had been a long, long time ago. In a whole different part of the world.

The trail descended and the shooter branched off to his right, reconnected with the main path and soon found his vehicle.

It was the only one in the makeshift parking area.

After stowing the rifle and gear, the shooter checked the satellite phone.

No surprise there.

A message from the man paying the bills.

It was pretty clear.

This mission is not over.

CHAPTER FIVE

The dishonorable discharge prevented any kind of formal military recognition at Nate Figueroa's funeral. It was a simple ceremony, attended by a few people, on a cold, rainy day in Minnesota.

The thick sheet of gray reminded Michael Tallon of how lucky he was to live in the desert. The blue sky, present nearly every single day, was an affirmation of life.

Tallon had grown up in rural Indiana where basketball was everything. He'd been a natural athlete, but football was where he'd excelled. Although a competent student, he'd been bored with studies and classrooms, even though he was an avid reader outside of school. He'd been transfixed by stories of men in far off countries fighting, loving, and sometimes dying.

So he'd joined the military and never looked back.

Until now.

Figueroa had been his brother. Not by blood in the traditional sense, but by blood in the literal sense. They'd seen their share of battlefields, saved each other's lives multiple times, and returned back to their home country with plenty of scars, and enough money in the bank to allow them the freedom to pursue their life's passion.

For Tallon, it had been to continue what he had been doing but on a much smaller, much less dangerous scale.

For Figueroa, it had eventually been to fight his most epic battle ever. Against cancer.

It had been the briefest of battles. From initial diagnosis to the end in a matter of weeks.

Figueroa must not have seen it coming.

And when he did, it was too late.

Tallon hadn't even known his friend had been sick. The news hit him like a sucker punch.

Now, Tallon watched as Figueroa's family gathered after the funeral. A few with umbrellas, waiting for cars to arrive to carry them back to the house and celebrate what they knew about their son, brother and husband.

Tallon wouldn't be joining them.

He'd already offered his condolences.

Paid his respects.

Said his final goodbye to one of the finest brothers he'd ever known.

Tallon checked the sky again.

It was still a solid sheet of gray.

No sign at all that somewhere behind the wall of darkness was a sun, trying to break through, but failing.

Forced to simply bide its time.

CHAPTER SIX

Pauling sat on the couch in her living room, staring at the phone in her hand.

A voice had just told her Reacher was dead.

It was like being told the Earth was flat after all.

Impossible.

Jack Reacher dead?

Pauling felt a dull thud in the pit of her stomach. A void opened up within her and she was surprised by the reaction. It had been a fair amount of time since she'd seen Reacher, yet she thought of him often. Wondered where he was, what he was doing, if he was ever going to stop by and see her again. As always, it was a train of thought that always ended at the same place: not likely.

Reacher was a wanderer, a traveler, a rogue. It was a spirit and a frame of mind that naturally resisted constraint.

Some people were simply born for the open road. Reacher was one of them. Maybe the very personification of that innate wanderlust.

Now Pauling faced the possibility that he was gone.

Reacher dead?

"Who is this?" she said into the phone.

There was silence on the other end of the line.

On a most basic level, Pauling obviously knew that everyone dies. Some much sooner than others. Sometimes, death arrives as a surprise. Other times, it's the end to a long period of suffering.

No one is immune.

Yet the idea that Jack Reacher was dead just didn't sit well with Pauling. He seemed so immovable, like a cosmic force that just...*was*.

The most obvious questions came to Pauling's mind. How had he died?

An accident?

Illness?

The questions raced through her mind like bullets from a machine gun.

"Hello?" Pauling said into the phone, this time with an edge in her voice.

She listened.

Thought she heard someone shift slightly.

"The body's at a town called Pine Beach, on Whidbey Island, near Deception Pass," the voice on the other end of the line finally said.

Something about the voice triggered suspicion in Pauling. The voice was too perfect. Scratchy. Gender-neutral. A neat, even cadence.

It was mechanical.

As in, processed.

"Who the hell are you—"

Pauling knew she had little chance of getting her question across in time, and she was right.

The line made a popping sound and she was disconnected.

Pauling again looked at the phone in her hand. The

number was blocked. She hit redial anyway but the call
wouldn't go through.

She set the phone down in frustration and picked up her
wine glass, got to her feet.

It was clearly a crank call. If Reacher was dead, she probably would have heard about it from someone in law enforcement. Her contacts or friends who knew she'd worked with
Reacher before.

And if someone did call her, it wouldn't be done this way.
Like some weird anonymous sex pervert.

And if it was a hoax, what was the point?

Did someone want to lure her to this town called Pine
Beach? And was using the idea that Jack Reacher was dead to
motivate her?

Or maybe she was convincing herself of a conspiracy
because she didn't want to face a horrible prospect.

That Jack Reacher really was dead.

Pauling thought about her next move as she went into the
kitchen and dumped the rest of her wine down the drain.

Sure, she could hop on a plane and be on her way.

But she was an investigator, first and foremost.

Occasionally, she had considered trying to track Reacher
down. To see him again. But she never had, because she felt
like she knew him well enough to understand that wasn't in
his plans. She could have forced the issue, but there would
have been no point.

Now, she had a reason to try to find him. A legitimate
one, not born out of loneliness and, frankly, lust.

Hopefully, she would be able to find him.

Alive.

CHAPTER SEVEN

The shooter paid cash for an anonymous beige sedan and drove to northern California. It was better than flying. Easier than renting a car. The right dealership, the proper amount of financial persuasion, and a complete absence of paperwork.

It also meant that all of the shooter's gear could be used for the next job. Ordinarily, that wasn't the best way to go. Better to ditch a hot weapon from the last job, start fresh with the next one.

But time was tight.

Besides, the killer was used to traveling and rarely got hassled by cops. Just drive the proper speed limit, avoid doing anything stupid, and everything would be fine.

The fee for these two jobs was crazy money.

The kind that lets a professional in this particular industry take a couple of years off, or, properly invested, maybe even retire.

The shooter had no intention of doing that, however. Too much time off and rust sets in. The eyes don't stay as sharp. The reflexes start to slow.

In this business, that was how a person retired early, as in permanent retirement.

The rifle in the trunk was a factory model, paid for with cash and sans paperwork. The weapon was mostly factory with a few modifications. This made it not only cheaper, but almost impossible to trace. It was a well-known brand whose civilian models were very popular with deer hunters. Hundreds of thousands of the rifles were sold every year.

It was a fine weapon, with a smooth action, devastating power and perfect accuracy.

The shooter had just proven that on a lonely road on Whidbey Island.

It was a long day's drive but the shooter made it to his location, settled in and spent the night.

At the appropriate time the next day, it was time to fulfill the last part of the contract.

Now, the shooter sighted the target, adjusted for the very slight east-to-west breeze and waited.

It wasn't a difficult shot.

The shooter had made many, many more difficult ones under high duress. This was a soft target, no one shooting back. The only difficulty was evasion and escape.

But that wasn't a problem, either.

Civilian police forces weren't really designed to quickly identify and apprehend a long-distance shooter. Certainly not a professional one with a military background.

Overconfidence and arrogance were the twin engines on the flight to failure, however. A professional knew that. The wrong street cop showing up at just the wrong time could ruin everything.

So necessary precautions had been taken.

Always plan.

Always prepare.

Always be ready to walk away.

But today, there wouldn't be any walking away.

Especially for the target.

Everything was ready. The evacuation vehicle and route were in place, all designed to avoid any areas with security cameras. There would be no eyewitnesses.

And there would be very little evidence left at the scene. But the professional knew that on a microscopic level, there was always something that would remain.

But all precautions had been taken to make sure none of it could be traced back.

Now, nearly two thousand yards away, there was movement.

The shooter eased into position with steadied breathing and waited.

Fifteen seconds later, the trigger was pulled.

CHAPTER EIGHT

To do the necessary research, Pauling left her apartment, and crossed over to West 4th Street where her office building was just around the corner.

She climbed the narrow staircase to her second floor office suite. Pauling unlocked the door and went inside. There was a waiting room in the front and then a second room that housed her office, which consisted of a desk, a computer, two visitors' chairs and a low cabinet with drawers that doubled as file cabinets.

Everything was sleek, modern and upper tier corporate design. Not outlandishly expensive, but not cheap, either. Most of Pauling's clients were high-income types, and her office reflected that.

She fired up her computer, zipped through her email and electronically filed anything outstanding.

And then she began to pursue Jack Reacher electronically.

There was really only one way, and she knew what it was.

Reacher carried an ATM card, a toothbrush, and a little bit of cash.

No way to trace a toothbrush or cash.

The ATM card, however, was another matter.

Pauling knew Reacher didn't spend much money on a daily basis. In fact, his biggest expenditures were coffee, and a change of clothes. The coffee he bought every day, the clothes, every few weeks or so.

Reacher lived easily and cheaply, always on the move.

Still, she figured he would need to replenish his cash occasionally, even though he hitched rides and stayed in cheap hotels.

Pauling estimated that if he lived frugally, he would still need to get cash at least once every few months, more or less depending on the level of his activity and where he was. If he was in a major city, it could be difficult to keep daily expenses down, as opposed to some small town in the middle of North Dakota where coffee and a huge breakfast came to a total of seven bucks or so.

It helped that Pauling had gotten to know Reacher on an intimate level, and even gotten a glimpse of his ATM card, so she knew which bank to sneak her way into. She hoped he hadn't changed banks for some reason. Pauling guessed he hadn't. Reacher was a guy who liked to keep things simple. If it wasn't broken, no need to fix it.

Armed with more knowledge than she usually had to work with, Pauling quickly slipped into the database of Reacher's bank. It was low-level hacking, essentially an open door left for Pauling by one of her former clients.

Pauling located Reacher's account with efficiency and noted his transactions. Small withdrawals, spread out sporadically every two to three months, ranging all across the country.

She noted with wry amusement, and maybe a touch of hurt feelings, that he had been near New York almost six months ago. But he hadn't reached out to contact her.

Oh well, she thought and continued to study the withdrawals.

Pauling let out a long breath.

His last withdrawal had been in Seattle.

Less than a week ago.

The mechanical voice on the phone had told her Reacher's body was near a town called Pine Beach, on Whidbey Island.

Pauling knew that Whidbey Island was in the Pacific Northwest, just north of Seattle, less than an hour by car.

For the first time, Pauling considered something that was difficult for her to even imagine.

Jack Reacher.

Dead.

CHAPTER NINE

Tallon pushed himself in the desert. It was his place of solace. His chair in front of a therapist. His temple.

The sun bore down on him with merciless intensity as he ran. The hills of Independence Springs were brown and barren to the naked eye. If one paused, life was abundant, it just didn't appear that way.

Tallon ran the long loop, a distance of nearly nineteen miles.

As with his body, his mind also ran free. And it turned to thoughts of Nate Figueroa. Tallon still couldn't believe his friend was gone. No warning. No word. Here one day, dead the next.

It happened before, of course. In his line of work, people died. Plain and simple. Some of them were men he knew slightly. Others, like Figueroa, were brothers-in-arms who'd fought, bled, and bonded on the battlefield.

It was never easy.

The experience always made Tallon take a step back and challenge his approach not only to work, but also to life.

The miles cruised by as Tallon's running rhythm comforted his thought process, made him feel like he could run forever. He'd made that mistake before, though. It was tempting to push on and add miles, but restraint in training was essential.

By the time he closed the loop and arrived at his predetermined stopping point, he was covered in sweat. His water was nearly gone and he walked the rest of the way back to his compound.

Tallon had carefully chosen the site that would come to be his home. It was a small ranch, or a casita, as the locals called it, roughly halfway between Los Angeles and Las Vegas. It wasn't visible from any main road or highway, and it afforded excellent protection.

The community was a modest size, but still big enough to provide anonymity, thanks to a fair percentage of the population being snowbirds who only flocked to the area during the winter months. Come April or May, they would lock up their homes or condos and head north.

Tallon lived at the place year-round. The hotter the better, in his opinion.

Building his casita had required a fair amount of time and a hefty budget, mostly because of the special requirements demanded by a man in his line of work.

There were multiple security cameras, some visible, some camouflaged. An elaborate security system with two backup generators. An underground armory, accessible only by a palm scanner.

There was a weightlifting room that occupied a space next to the garage and the landscaping had been chosen carefully.

Instead of arranging the plants to orchestrate a year-round bloom, Tallon's needs focused on preventing cover for an attacking force while also providing clear shooting lanes for someone inside the structure.

Tallon had also spared no expense on the communication system. There was a hardwired landline, buried. A wireless radio unit. Two satellite phones with multiple batteries and chargers. A hardwired communication system for cable and Internet, along with a satellite-based stream that could continue to feed the home information without power and if the physical cables were somehow severed.

The windows were bulletproof, the entry doors made of specific construction materials designed to withstand explosives and high-impact rounds.

It wasn't that Tallon had a large number of enemies. It was all about the high-level capabilities of people who could, in theory, seek to find Tallon for reasons counter to his health.

Now, before he entered the house, Tallon checked his security screens, and then used the facial recognition scanner to unlock the back door to the casita.

Inside, he took a long, hot shower before heading to the kitchen for an enormous glass of cold iced tea.

Tallon took the drink into his home office, and settled into a leather club chair that featured a laptop perched on a swivel desktop. As he sipped his tea, he perused the Internet, and checked his email.

Not much in the email folders, and even less on the news websites and military blogs he followed.

It wasn't until he was going to close his browser, that Tallon noticed his spam folder.

It had the number 1 in bold in parentheses.

There was a little line next to the parentheses that read 'empty now.'

Tallon brought his cursor over and was about to click on

the 'empty now' but he didn't. His finger hovered there for a moment.

Many times, he would look back and wonder what would have happened, or what would not have happened, if he'd just emptied the spam folder without opening it.

But he didn't.

He clicked the folder and an email appeared in the main window.

It was from an address he had never seen before.

The subject line was empty.

The body of the email was simple.

They followed us. –F.

Tallon sat there, stunned.

F.

Figueroa?

CHAPTER TEN

The Senator from the great state of Oklahoma was Noah Raskins, the great grandson of a wildcatter and the spitting image of a riverboat gambler. He wore expensive striped suits, sported a thick moustache and had one of the largest and most valuable cowboy hat collections in the world.

He was in northern California for a conference with Oklahoma's Economic Development Council. It seemed someone had decided a vineyard in California might be an excellent investment for the state of Oklahoma. Wine was bigger than ever. All sorts of fancy wine subscription services were taking off, and some wine-drinking politician had a brilliant idea.

When he'd gotten the invite, Raskins had smiled. He knew there would be no purchase of a California vineyard.

Not in a million years.

Raskins imagined the howling that would ensue if the purchase was made, once some enterprising journalist got ahold of it.

No, the state of Oklahoma would most definitely not be buying a vineyard in California.

However, the most important aspect of that for Raskins and the other men (no women allowed) had nothing to do with purchasing.

No, it had to do with research.

And for that, the state of Oklahoma would unequivocally pay.

The entire trip, lodgings, and per diem were all being footed by taxpayers.

The men assembled were going to have a great time, get drunk, and maybe see if there were any ladies available for some additional entertainment.

Raskins also had to smile because the vineyard was actually for sale. And it might even be purchased by some members of his group, but it would be handled privately, by a member or two of the council, with maybe a few silent partners, such as Raskins himself, through a private investment group with no public ties to anyone at the vineyard.

He almost laughed again. Research!

A bunch of good ol' boys sitting around a giant fireplace in some lodge in California, drinking wine and scotch, getting absolutely shit-faced. And it was all a taxpayer-funded boondoggle.

The spoils of victory, he thought to himself. All those years out pounding the flesh, making speeches, listening to "real" folk bitch about their problems. He'd put in his time, that was for certain.

The fact was, he hated real people. Oh, he had a great touch with the locals. They loved him.

But there was a reason they were "little" people. A lack of skills. A lack of intelligence. A lack of drive.

They were at their current station in life thanks to their own doing. He wasn't about to blame himself for being a cut above.

Way above, he corrected himself.

So what was wrong with a getaway to wine country?

Hell, half the senators in Washington hired hookers as "staff." Nothing like having Joe Taxpayer pony up the cash for your pussy. Now that was a little over the top, Raskins thought, even though he'd been guilty of the practice a time or two. Maybe three.

Now, as the tall Oklahoman stepped out onto the porch of the vineyard's lodge, he took a moment to soak in the fading California sun. It wasn't hot out here like in Oklahoma, he thought.

Not as humid, either.

In his home state, it didn't matter if you were in the sun or the shade, the heat and cloying dampness was the same.

Back home, he would be sweat–

A slight movement in the distance made Raskins pause. He had excellent eyesight. His pale blue eyes were notorious for being able to pick out distant mule deer on a hunt in the mountains.

So his train of thought was interrupted by something vague in the distance.

And then his mind was permanently interrupted by the bullet that crashed through the center of his forehead and blew apart most of his head.

Later, the mayor of a small town in Oklahoma who'd managed to get invited on the "business trip" to the vineyard, would remember Noah Raskin's cowboy hat. The mayor had been standing just inside the vineyard's lodge, watching Raskins stand on the porch like he owned the place.

He would tell the story for years to come, how Raskins' cowboy hat suddenly popped up into the air and hovered for the briefest moment, while the senator's brains were splattered all over the wooden floor.

No one heard the shot, they only saw its aftermath.

Senator Noah Raskins, dead on the porch of a vineyard in California.

Shot by a sniper.

His three thousand dollar cowboy hat?

Not a mark on it.

CHAPTER ELEVEN

Pine Beach. Deception Pass.

The names meant nothing to Pauling. She'd heard of Whidbey Island, only because she knew there was a military base there, and at some point she'd been in Seattle and someone had referenced the base.

But Pine Beach, the town where Reacher's body was found, was unfamiliar to her. Where it was in location to the military base, she had no idea.

Pauling sat in her office and contemplated the next move.

She certainly had no intention of hopping on a plane and flying across the country to find out this was all someone's idea of a sick joke.

Not when she had a cell phone and the contact information for Pine Beach Police Department, Whidbey Island. It was on the screen of her laptop and she punched in the number.

After several rings, a male voice answered, sounding tired.

"Pine Beach PD," he said.

"My name is Lauren Pauling and I'm calling because I was notified that a body was found in or near your jurisdiction."

There was silence on the other end of the line.

"I was told the victim was identified as Jack Reacher," Pauling continued. "Can you confirm or deny this?"

"Uh, hold on," the voice said.

Pauling wasn't impressed so far with the Pine Beach, PD. But she reserved judgment. Maybe the guy was an intern.

There was an abrupt click on the line and Pauling was certain the operator had disconnected her, but then another voice spoke on the line.

"This is Chief Jardine," the voice said. "With whom am I speaking?"

The speaker was female, and Pauling could sense the annoyance in the woman's tone.

"Lauren Pauling."

A pause and Pauling heard the sound of pen on paper. Taking notes. Always a good idea. She was doing the same.

"You have some information for me?" Jardine asked. "Is that correct?"

Pauling almost smiled at the woman's attempt to put her on the defensive. "Not exactly. I received a call that a deceased person was found in your jurisdiction. ID'd as a man named Jack Reacher. I was calling to confirm."

There was a sigh on the other end of the line. "I'm afraid it doesn't work that way, Ms. Pauling," the chief said. "Are you family? Related to this man you mentioned?"

"Not exactly," Pauling admitted.

"Okay, well, even if parts of what you say may or may not be true, we would never give out any kind of information like that over the phone," Jardine said. "We do have some questions for you, though."

"I'm in New York, Chief Jardine," Pauling said. "I'm sure there's nothing I can tell you."

"Sure there is," the woman said, suddenly sounding cheerful. Almost like a chirp.

Pauling waited.

"For starters," Jardine said. "Who the hell is Jack Reacher?"

CHAPTER TWELVE

They followed us.

Tallon couldn't make sense of the message.

Who did?

He sat in front of his computer, the iced tea forgotten.

Behind him, the television was on, and the announcers were talking about the murder of Senator Noah Raskins of Oklahoma.

"I'll be damned," Tallon said. He'd never met Raskins, but he'd heard plenty of stories about him. A member of multiple committees on military issues, Raskins was known to most of the armed forces.

Not much was known.

It was clearly murder.

A gunshot from some distance.

A sniper? Tallon wondered. Now that would certainly ratchet up the intrigue.

From stories he'd heard, Tallon figured that if it was true Raskins was murdered it would either be from somebody he screwed in a shady business deal, or a woman he screwed on his desk in the Senate.

It was too early for any actual information and after about ten minutes the news coverage began to repeat itself, so Tallon shut off the television. He enjoyed the quiet more, anyway.

Besides, he wanted to wrestle some more with the email from Figueroa.

They followed us.

It made no sense.

Tallon and Figueroa had done a lot of work together. Both officially in the military, and unofficially for various employers.

They weren't mercenaries, per se. They had standards and never worked for anyone who was clearly on the wrong side of humanity.

But they had been very busy.

Their skills were always in high demand.

The thing was, it seemed impossible for Tallon to imagine anyone following them. They were nearly always strangers in a strange land. Faceless. Nameless. Without a country. Without allegiances.

And had Figueroa actually sent the email?

He'd clearly been very sick. That was the thing with electronic communication like email, you didn't always know for sure who was on the other end.

He thought back to over a year ago, the last time he'd seen Figueroa.

It had been a bad mission, in a bad place, with some very bad people involved.

They followed us.

Tallon went into his kitchen, grabbed a beer and peered out into the dark desert landscape.

He thought about the missions he had shared with Figueroa. There were so many it was nearly impossible to count. They'd fought side-by-side in Africa, Indonesia, South America, Mexico and at various spots in Europe.

Most had been successful, others had resulted in an imperfect solution.

None of them had been abject failures.

The other thing that stuck in Tallon's mind was the idea that someone had followed them. Generally, the bad guys they targeted on missions weren't left alive. Harsh, he knew.

But dead men tend not to have the option of following their killers around. Unless they're ghosts hoping to haunt guilty consciences.

Tallon didn't have a guilty conscience.

And he certainly didn't believe in ghosts.

One word repeated itself in his mind.

Impossible.

CHAPTER THIRTEEN

Back-to-back contracts were not the ideal way to work. Normally, there would be a need to take some time off, clear the head, get back in the zone. But this had been a special case. Or two special cases, as it were.

Although luck was never really involved in this line of work, the first project had been fortunate. Relatively easy, although there was hesitation to use that term when it came to the profession of killing human beings. The actual process might be simple, but the stakes were high, so it would never be considered easy.

But compared to other jobs, the first one had definitely been without complications. A lone man, walking near the forest. Multiple evacuation routes. Plenty of opportunity to scout the location, make sure no witnesses were present before, during or after. No security cameras.

Law enforcement nowhere nearby.

A good, clean kill.

The second one had been a doozy.

A much more populated kill zone. Plenty of witnesses. Several evacuation routes to choose from, however, most of them had a fair amount of traffic. Law enforcement was definitely present, along with the senator's private security detail.

It had been a huge planning process. It had required a trip to the winery, armed with the target's travel itinerary, and a thorough job of preliminary scouting. Then a return to the site of the second job to scout it, and execute the mission.

Afterward, it was back to the second project, and make the kill.

The intensity of the planning for both jobs, along with the added stress of the high-profile second target, had created fatigue.

But also an edge.

Whenever the job was finished, it always did the same thing.

Hole up in an expensive hotel, and book a high-priced escort from the most expensive service of its kind.

Quality was essential.

And worth the price.

Now, the blonde entered the hotel suite. He was young, but well-built, dressed in cotton shorts and a form-fitting short-sleeved shirt. Probably linen.

The shooter who had just assassinated a senator, smiled at the escort's reaction. He had probably been expecting an ugly, overweight business woman desperate for male companionship.

She must have been a surprise to him.

Small. Petite. Red hair and a slim, but rock-hard body.

He smiled at her.

She smiled back.

Walked toward him.

She had earned this prize.

And now, she was going to make sure he earned his money, too.

"Get on your knees," she said to him.

CHAPTER FOURTEEN

L auren Pauling firmly believed in experiences over objects.

She was not the type to obsess over luxury vehicles, expensive jewelry (to a point) or engage in competitive real estate acquisition.

BSOs, a.k.a. bright shiny objects, tended not to hold much allure for her.

However, comfort was a different matter.

It had nothing to do with prestige, but when Pauling had worked for the FBI, travel was often highly unglamorous. Budget-friendly, as her coworkers liked to say. Cheap hotel rooms. Second-rate rental cars. Less than stellar restaurants due to a small government per diem.

So now, when Pauling traveled on business, it was her business. And she gladly paid for comfort.

Nearing fifty, Pauling was in great shape and stretched her legs, enjoying the extra room in first-class. An unopened bottled water sat on her tray table, and she toyed with the idea of ordering a Blood Mary, then decided against it.

Instead, she took out her laptop and fired up her browser.

Pine Beach was a small community on Whidbey Island, which sat in Puget Sound just north of Seattle. Pauling had been to Seattle many times, and had even driven north on I-5 into Vancouver, Canada. Beautiful, rugged country, she recalled. She'd never been on Whidbey Island, though.

Was it where Jack Reacher died?

Pauling shook the thought from her mind.

Too soon to jump to conclusions. She had to admit though, the remoteness and ruggedness of the place would have drawn Reacher to it. She could imagine him hitchhiking along the single highway that cut through the middle of Whidbey Island. Looking for a diner for a strong cup of black coffee. Maybe someone in trouble who needed help.

Reacher always looked out for the little guy.

It was one of the things about him that fascinated her. It just seemed like there weren't men like Reacher around anymore.

He was one of a kind.

While Reacher was more than happy to stick a thumb out for a ride, there would be no hitching rides for Pauling.

She would land in Seattle, get a rental car and make the drive. She checked her watch. By her estimation she would be in Pine Beach around dinnertime.

It would give her an opportunity to talk to Chief Jardine face-to-face, as the phone conversation hadn't been very effective.

Later, she would check into her hotel room and grab a bite to eat.

Pauling connected to her airline Wi-Fi account, for which she paid a premium. Her plan was to take a quick peek at the best restaurants in Pine Beach.

Instead, a breaking news article popped onto her screen.

Senator Noah Raskins had been assassinated.

Pauling looked at the photo of the man.

She knew him.

For a brief, fleeting moment, she remembered that he had been a prominent part of certain military committees and her mind connected it with the body of a man who may or may not be Jack Reacher.

Pauling saw in the story that the senator had been shot in California.

She subtly scolded herself. There was no way someone killed Jack Reacher in Washington and then shot a prominent senator the next day.

No way.

For starters, she had no idea if the body was Jack Reacher. And secondly, she had no idea if he'd been hit by a car, or stabbed, or fallen off a cliff.

So there was no reason to try to connect the two.

Pauling laughed at herself. What the hell? Was she becoming a conspiracy theorist?

She shut her laptop.

Maybe it was time to have that Bloody Mary after all.

CHAPTER FIFTEEN

I t was no accident that the wealthiest city in Europe was home to a group of men and women who called themselves the Zurich Collective.

They had formed themselves decades ago and seen some changes throughout their existence. Members had come and gone, mostly due to death. It was rare for an individual to leave while healthy and even more uncommon for them to leave on their own volition.

Members joked the only way out was feet first.

While the organization had seen some changes, its current lineup was its most powerful, ever. Which was an impressive feat, given that past configurations had accomplished feats including altering the global economy, manipulating outcomes in world wars and overthrowing a dozen governments in countries spanning the globe.

The current group was neatly divided into two constituencies.

The first were the ultra wealthy. Titans of commerce, heads of multinational companies, independent sellers of black-market goods and services.

The second group wasn't quite as wealthy as the first, but were paid huge sums by various employers to protect mutual assets and business interests.

They shared a level playing field within the association, however.

Save for one.

Her name was Gunnella Bohm, and she was a towering figure both literally and figuratively. Standing 6'3" tall with broad shoulders, solid hips and a hawk nose, she ran the Zurich Collective with a precision that rivaled the region's world-renowned watchmakers.

Other than her legendary sexual appetite, Gunnella Bohm was known for her extraordinary wealth and passion for increasing that wealth at all costs. She consumed power like she consumed lovers; with great vigor and with a goal of wringing everything useful from her target before moving on.

Her wealth was both inherited and earned. Her father, a German industrialist, had been stripped of a great deal of his assets due to his sympathies for the Nazi party. However, he had been able to squirrel away nearly a quarter of his wealth by hiding it in various banks scattered throughout mostly South America.

When he died, as his only heir, Gunnella Bohm reassembled that small slice of the family pie and proceed to grow it with a shrewdness and ruthlessness that far surpassed her father's reputation for both.

She had also replaced his spot on the Zurich Collective and it soon became apparent to all that even among them, she was something special. Within ten years of joining the collective, she was made its presumptive head.

Now, she turned from the enormous window that looked out over Lake Zurich and faced the others in the room. They were seated along a long table made of tempered glass. The walls were white, the video screen at the end of the table was sheathed in chrome. Several glass pitchers of water were placed in intervals along the length of the table, but no one had bothered to accept a glass.

"That brings us to America," she said. "Gregory. Give us your situation report."

Heads turned toward a petite man sporting a silk suit and a delicate face. He had black hair just beginning to pepper with gray and he spoke with a highly articulated, high-pitched voice.

"Our objective was achieved with no negative consequences," he said. "I continue to monitor the situation, but as of now I anticipate no issues."

"Is the scale of the initial investigation what you expected?" Bohm pressed. Other heads along the table raised slightly at the follow-up question.

It was never a good sign.

"Of course," Gregory said. "When a senator is murdered, they pull out all the stops. But initial reports continue to indicate the lack of evidence. Investigators are stymied and I see no reason why that should change."

Gunnella Bohm studied Gregory's face.

She had spent a lifetime perfecting the art of interpreting facial and body mechanics. Something in Gregory's pursed lips made her wonder if he really did have everything under control.

Immediately, Gunnella Bohm made plans to safeguard the situation.

Any deviations from the plan in the United States would need to be dealt with quickly, and if needed, with violence.

It was the only way.

There was simply too much at stake.

CHAPTER SIXTEEN

"Shoot him," Figueroa looked at Tallon.

"No, please," the man seated on the ground said, with his hands cuffed behind his back. He was sweating, and his eyes were wide with fear. But both Tallon and Figueroa saw beyond the fear. They saw something else.

Resistance.

Arrogance.

Cunning.

The fear was real, Tallon knew. He just wasn't sure if their captive was afraid of them, or his boss.

Ferdinand Sica.

Gunfire chattered nearby and Tallon and Figueroa both swiveled, Tallon's gun still pointed at their captive's forehead.

"Where is he?" Tallon asked the man on the ground.

"Shoot him," Figueroa repeated. "He's not going to tell us."

An explosion rocked the ground beneath them, and over the tops of the trees ahead, a thick column of black smoke rose into the sky.

"He'll be on the chopper by now," the man said, shaking his head. And then he smiled. "You stupid gringos will never catch him."

Figueroa stepped back and cracked the man on top of the skull with the butt of his rifle. The man toppled over onto his side.

"Jackass," Figueroa said to the unconscious man.

Tallon cursed under his breath. He raced ahead, knowing the team was counting on them to cut Sica off before he could get to any form of transportation.

Tallon was fairly sure the man had been bluffing. They had done a thorough job of scouting and there was virtually no way Sica could have made it to the chopper already.

As he ran, he reconsidered their objective.

There were only six members of the squad assigned to this mission, and Tallon feared the amount of gunfire he'd heard was not good news. He also recognized the sounds for what they were. The team all had similar weapons, and much of the gunfire was not coming from them. Which meant their opposition was still alive and armed.

Not good.

Smoke filled the air, more gunfire erupted and another explosion sounded off behind the fortress. The sky, already overcast, now held clouds of smoke and Tallon's nostrils burned with the scent of fire and gasoline.

A chopper's engine whined above the din and Tallon increased his pace, running to the left of the compound's concrete wall.

He rounded the corner, Figueroa hot on his heels.

Tallon saw three armed men waving two small figures toward a chopper. One of Tallon's men was already down, and he couldn't see the others.

Tallon lifted his rifle and felt a hammer blow to his shoulder that spun him around and dropped him to the ground. He continued to roll, heard and felt the bullets tear up ground behind him.

Figueroa was down on one knee, firing at the chopper.

Tallon fired as well, saw the three armed men now down, and he poured his rounds into the chopper, watching the helicopter's glass *dome shatter underneath the rounds, and the two smaller figures were down on the ground, as well.*

Suddenly, there was silence.

A burning sensation tore at Tallon's shoulder but he ignored it as he got to his feet and ran toward the chopper. Figueroa was behind him.

The figures on the ground were dead. Blood everywhere. Body parts still smoking.

Tallon went to the two smaller individuals who'd been running toward the chopper.

The first was their target, Ferdinand Sica. The biggest active narco trafficker in the world.

Now dead.

The second figure's face was covered.

Tallon brushed the black scarf aside.

Caught his breath.

A girl.

CHAPTER SEVENTEEN

Pauling had her choice of vehicles in the premium, members-only portion of the car rental lot. As a member of the loyalty program, there was no waiting at the check-out counter.

You went to the rental car lot, saw your name on a board, and were free to pick any vehicle in that area.

The keys were already inside.

Along with the paperwork.

Pauling made her way to the designated area where an Audi SUV caught her eye. All-wheel drive probably wasn't a bad idea out here, considering the mountains.

She threw her bag into the back seat, got behind the wheel and exited the parking structure after showing her ID.

The Pacific Northwest's reputation for gray skies and clouds proved to be well-earned. There was a layer of gunmetal across the dark sky. The Seattle skyline faded into Pauling's rearview mirror as she headed north toward Whidbey Island.

After she threaded her way through the glut of traffic near

the airport and then downtown, Pauling was free to let her mind wander as the roads opened up.

She hoped this was all a big misunderstanding, that the person they had in the morgue was not Jack Reacher.

One, she hated the thought that Reacher was gone. Somehow, she had always envisioned a scenario where she would see him again. Probably foolish, but maybe not. She was former FBI. He was a former Army investigator specializing in homicides. They had ended up working together on a criminal case.

It happened once.

It could happen again.

Pauling just wasn't ready to accept that Reacher was gone. The idea that he was out there somewhere, armed with nothing but an ATM card and toothbrush, gave her comfort. Injustice was everywhere. Every small town, big city, wherever people had to interact with other people, someone was probably getting taken advantage of. It was the way the world worked.

But for the lucky few being oppressed or victimized, Jack Reacher made things right.

Pauling struggled to stop her train of thought. Failing to keep an open mind, she was already convincing herself this was a fool's errand. A hoax.

She almost laughed at herself. Dropping everything, flying across the country based on very little information. On the bright side, maybe she could wrap this up in a couple of hours and not waste too much more time.

Pauling figured she could get to the bottom of the mystery, and then maybe zip down to Portland for a few days to visit her sister. It would be good to see her little nieces and nephews again. Maybe the little town of Pine Beach had some cute shops she could find a couple of toys for the kids. Wasn't it an aunt's job to spoil the kids?

Traffic was light as she pushed the Audi north, eventually swinging to the west and crossing onto Whidbey Island. The road was a narrow two-lane highway when she got to Deception Pass, a stunning bridge over a strait separating Whidbey Island from the next piece of land over. The water churned below, and steep cliffs opened out onto a wide expanse of water, bluffs and trees.

It was a sight, and Pauling felt a slight tinge of vertigo as she drove along the bridge, the feeling of emptiness beneath her.

The road wound through the rugged hills and eventually it flattened out and soon she was pulling into the town of Pine Beach.

It was on the water, naturally, and featured a main street that ran parallel to the widest part of the harbor. Evergreens surrounded the area and in the distance, a mountain range neatly framed the expansive view. On the water, a variety of boats, both pleasure and working, were either docked or in transit. Gulls flew overhead and the faint smell of fish filled the air.

Pauling had programmed in the police station's address and she found it at the end of town, set back from the water several blocks, set on a wide patch of land that was probably donated to the city. Not valuable in the least for anything commercial. Down the street from the police station were two other municipal buildings. One of them was a library, the other a small elementary school.

She pulled into a visitor parking spot, got out, and went inside.

It smelled like a library, a little bit musty, with an overlay of artificial evergreen scent, which amused Pauling. Why not just open a window?

A front desk, not separated from the lobby, sat facing the front door. No bulletproof glass here, Pauling noted. Not a lot of highly violent offenders coming in and out of the police station every day, she surmised.

Pauling stepped up to the desk, which was unmanned. She glanced around, wondering if she'd caught someone on a bathroom break.

"Can I help you?"

A uniformed officer glanced out from behind a filing cabinet.

"I'm here to see Chief Jardine. Lauren Pauling."

The face disappeared from view and Pauling heard the sound of a file drawer being rolled shut and moments later, a side door off the lobby opened.

"Follow me," the cop who'd been behind the filing cabinet said. He was young and his pants looked short, as if he'd just completed a growth spurt.

Pauling followed him down the hall and then he pointed to an office with glass walls and an open door. The cop veered left, and Pauling stuck her head in the door.

"Chief Jardine?"

A woman with dark hair, cut short, glanced up from a computer.

"You're Pauling?"

"Yes."

Chief Jardine nodded. Pauling studied the woman's face. It was all sharp angles and the eyes were small but shone with an intensity that seemed out of place in the low-key atmosphere of the office.

Jardine straightened up in her chair, took a long, appraising glance at Pauling.

"What do you say we start with the body?"

CHAPTER EIGHTEEN

As much as he wanted to do it over the phone, Tallon knew that wasn't an option. He reversed the flight he'd made days ago, and headed back to Minnesota.

The streets and neighborhood of Figueroa's family looked the same as from the funeral, but much more sad with all of the people gone.

The presence of many was the point of funerals, Tallon supposed. A way of coping with loss.

Now, returning to the place of grief, the quiet was especially powerful.

He parked his rental in front of the Figueroa house and walked to the front door. It was a modest structure, a craftsman-style bungalow with a wide front porch and a center gable that looked out onto the street. There were two chairs and a cocktail table on the porch near the corner. Tallon pictured his friend sitting there with his father, drinking beers, talking about some of Nate's exploits.

Now, the chairs were empty, and wet with the rain that had passed through the area.

The doorbell appeared to be broken so he knocked. It was early evening. Well after the day's work should be done but also at a time where interrupting dinner might be a possibility.

It was cold. The damp chill in the air seemed to penetrate Tallon's clothing.

He had packed quickly and the chilled Minnesota air cut through the thin denim jacket he had on. If he'd taken a little more time and not made such a hasty departure for the airport, he would have added a few more layers to his suitcase.

The front door was solid wood, not surprising on a house that had to have been built not much less than a hundred years earlier. It was a densely populated neighborhood. The homes were small but tidy. Lawns were cut. No signs of peeled paint. A neighborhood with pride.

The heavy door opened and Tallon found himself looking at Figueroa's father. A shorter, stockier version of his friend, with gray hair and a face that had aged since he'd last seen it, just a few days back.

"Help you?" Charles Figueroa asked.

"I'm Michael Tallon, I was a friend of Nate's," he said. "I was here just a few days ago for the funeral."

Recognition dawned on the older man's face.

"Oh, yes. I remember you. I'm sorry, come in," he said. He stepped aside and Tallon entered the home.

"Coffee? I know it's late, but you look like you're cold."

"Yeah, I'd love a cup, thanks," Tallon said. He followed the older man down the hallway into the house. It was well-kept. Area rugs, dark wood floors and comfortable furniture. In the kitchen, Charles Figueroa grabbed two cups, filled them, and gestured toward the living room, where he took the center spot on a leather couch, and pointed Tallon toward a club chair.

"What can I do for you?" the older man asked.

Tallon took a deep breath. He'd thought about this on the plane ride and had decided that the best way forward was to be honest.

"When I got back home after the funeral, I found a strange email from Nate," Tallon said. "It simply said 'they followed us.' I'm kind of confused by it, because it appears that it was sent after Nate had passed away. So I'm wondering if someone else may have sent it, and if you know who that might be." He had printed off a copy of the email and handed it to his old friend's father. Charles Figueroa looked at the sheet, read it several times and handed it back.

"Well, I know that's Nate's email address," the older man said. "I got the hang of email a few years back. But I don't know what that message might have meant. And I don't know who might have sent it, if it wasn't from Nate."

Tallon recognized honesty when he saw it.

"Nate may have sent it," Tallon said. "There's a way to schedule emails to go out after you've written them. I don't know how to do it, but I know it can be done. I'm just not sure why Nate would have done that."

The old man shrugged his shoulders, waited for Tallon to continue.

"Had anything happened before Nate became ill? Had he said anything or anyone was bothering him? Some issue that he was having?" Tallon asked. "I'm really sorry to ask, but this message really came out of the blue."

Charles Figueroa glanced down and to the left before he spoke.

"Oh, there are always issues in a family," he said. "Always."

Tallon nodded. It was hard for him to identify with the notion of family.

He was an only child, and both of his parents were gone.

He really didn't have much in the way of family, which is why the military had become a second home for him.

"I always considered Nate my brother. I hope he felt the same about me," Tallon said. And then waited.

"Nate has a sister up in Seattle," the older man said. He let out a long breath. "She called him and asked for help. He went out there and when he came back, he wasn't the same. Something was wrong. And then that was it."

Tallon's first thought was, *why didn't he call me?*

It was a selfish reaction.

"Nate's sister. Is she okay now?"

The old man looked up from the area rug he'd been studying.

"That's just it. No one can find her."

CHAPTER NINETEEN

The morgue was located in Coupeville, the seat of Island County, just a stone's throw from Pine Beach.

Jardine had verified Pauling's identity and background before she agreed to take her to the morgue, which was housed in a long, low-slung building that reminded Pauling of an elementary school.

Except this one had drawers for dead bodies, instead of pencils and erasers.

Chief Jardine vouched for her at the various security checkpoints and eventually, they made their way to the basement where a gurney was brought in to a viewing room.

"This one's going to be tricky," Jardine said. "You won't be able to do any kind of facial recognition, if you know what I mean. We couldn't even get dental records."

"So what do you want me to do?" Pauling asked.

"No surviving family members, so if you can at least recognize the body, that would be a good thing," Chief Jardine said. "At least it would be a place for us to start."

"How am I supposed to identify him if there's nothing of him...left?"

Jardine shrugged her shoulders. "I don't know. Maybe there were birthmarks? Scars? Some identifying marks on his body?"

Pauling was tempted to make a joke but it never really formulated in her mind. It had to do with the fact that she was intimately familiar with Jack Reacher's body. Had actually pictured it many, many times in her mind since their last time together. Maybe too many times.

"I can try," she said.

A man in a white lab coat pulled the sheet from an incredible specimen of the male body. A huge upper body with broad shoulders and chest, long, thick arms, down to a relatively narrow waist with big, strong legs.

The sheet was kept over what remained of the body above the neck.

From where she was standing, Pauling could see the chest and pec area. She knew Jack Reacher had various scars on his body. She had run her fingers, and maybe even her lips, along their patterns some time ago.

Pauling studied the body before her with great care. Jardine didn't say a word. The man in the lab coat just waited. Somewhere, a voice shouted outside the room and then it was silent again.

"May I take a closer look?" Pauling finally asked.

Chief Jardine gestured toward the body. "Be my guest."

Pauling walked closer to the body. Studied the legs. The waist. The flat stomach. The incredible chest and shoulders. The arms were enormous.

The dimensions seemed right.

She studied the scars.

Closed her eyes, tried to picture what she remembered of Reacher.

And then she opened them.

"It's him," she said.

CHAPTER TWENTY

Tallon was angry.

And hurt.

But they were emotions on which he rarely ever dwelled.

And this was no exception.

The fact that Figueroa, his de facto brother, hadn't told him about the illness was one thing. That, he could understand, to a degree. Illness, especially something like cancer, sometimes caused people to retreat into themselves. So Figueroa hadn't called him to let him know about his condition.

But Figueroa's sister was missing?

And he hadn't called Tallon to enlist his help?

Why not?

What could have possibly prevented him from doing so?

As he packed, he found solace in the act of compartmentalizing objects, and he transferred that approach to his emotions.

Having spent the vast majority of his adult life in the military, Tallon's way of living made packing for trips on short notice a matter of routine.

Within hours of his return from the Figueroa household in Minnesota, he had his SUV loaded with gear and supplies for the drive to Whidbey Island.

He could have simply hopped a plane from Minneapolis and flown directly to Seattle, but something told him it would be a good idea to bring along the kinds of resources that are prohibited on airlines.

Arming the compound was the most time-consuming task. It wasn't as simple as punching in a code on an alarm panel by the garage door. Tallon had special compartments and storage areas in the house that required extra steps to secure. Once he finished those, he activated the motion-detection system linked to a series of hidden cameras. The images were available for him to view on his smartphone, if he so desired.

Finally, loaded with food, water, clothes and a small but effective selection of weapons carefully stashed in a special section of his SUV, Tallon set out for Seattle.

It would be a lonely drive for much of the time. He would skirt Death Valley before eventually connecting with I-5 in northern California and from there, it would be a relatively straight shot through Oregon to Whidbey Island.

Plenty of time for him to think through what he'd learned in Minnesota.

It was a puzzle.

And not a good kind of mystery. His friend was dead and before his death, had been dealing with a problem. A problem he felt hadn't required Michael Tallon's assistance.

The road rose as it neared the mountains and Tallon felt the reassurance as his vehicle's beefy engine surged ahead, even sped up as the incline increased.

It was mid-morning and the sun was up, the sky was a

clear blue, and in the distance Tallon could see a hawk circling far overhead.

As he drove he cycled through a variety of scenarios, trying to better understand what kind of trouble Figueroa's sister might have been in, and how he would have approached it.

There just wasn't enough information for him to put any credence into his ideas. There was a good chance he would get there and it would turn out to be nothing. Maybe the sister had met some guy Figueroa hadn't approved of, and now she'd run off with him. End of story. Or maybe the sister had been surprised by a trip to Europe and hadn't had time to let everyone know.

Stranger things had happened.

If it did turn out to be a simple case of miscommunication, it would mean Tallon made an eleven-hour drive for no good reason.

Except driving down lonesome highways was something he enjoyed. He relished the open space. The lack of confinement. The anonymity.

Besides, it was his duty to find Figueroa's sister and make sure she was okay. Even though his friend hadn't asked him to.

Figueroa would have done the same for him.

The miles and hours flew by. Traffic remained sparse.

Soon, he was blazing through Oregon, then navigating his way up the Washington coast before finally hitting some urban congestion around Seattle. But it was well after rush-hour and he made short work of it.

He'd settled on a reasonably-priced hotel and self-parked the SUV. He brought his gear up to his room and checked his phone.

There was one unopened email.

He checked the sender.

Figueroa?
Impossible.
He opened it.
There was one word.
Sica.

CHAPTER TWENTY-ONE

There wasn't much to choose from in Pine Beach for lodging. Pauling had secretly hoped she would be on her way back to Seattle right then, but it was a no-go. After the scene in the morgue, she wanted to stay.

And drink.

She wasn't normally a drinker, but suddenly she wanted to feel the warm buzz from a couple glasses of wine. Or maybe a good, strong martini.

In any event, she found an overpriced but quaint hotel on the water and checked into her room, showered, and changed into jeans and a fleece pullover. Down by the bar there was a fireplace with a pair of leather chairs and a rough-hewn table. She ordered a dirty martini at the bar, sunk into the chair and when her drink was handed to her, she drank half of it in one long pull.

The fire was fake. A gas flame with artificial logs looking like a discarded prop from a B movie.

Oh well.

Why have a real fireplace in a location like this? Where

would you get firewood? It's not like the area was surrounded by towering pine trees or anything.

Sarcasm wasn't the place to go, Pauling thought to herself. Besides, it was kind of pointless when it was an audience of one.

Pauling took another drink of the martini and thought about what she'd seen. Not good. Not good at all. It had taken a very powerful rifle to do that kind of damage and create such difficulty in being able to identify the body.

The sight of that body, Pauling thought. She gave an imperceptible shake of her head, thought about her past with Jack Reacher.

They were good memories but in light of this situation, they felt like bad thoughts.

The last of her martini went down the hatch and Pauling popped the olive into her mouth. It had been stuffed with blue cheese.

It was good, but she couldn't have another one.

The server noticed her and Pauling asked for a glass of chardonnay.

Chief Jardine had seemed to be satisfied with her identification of Reacher. They'd exchanged business cards and Pauling was honest in telling her she was going to stay put for the night and probably leave in the morning.

Pauling wondered what it was like to be a female police chief in a place like this. It had the look of a town that would be filled with rugged lumberjacks on the weekends. Plaid shirts. Lots of facial hair. Plenty of drunk-and-disorderlies.

Rough-hewn folks who probably liked to get rough on the weekends.

Then again, Jardine seemed like she could take care of herself. A hard woman who looked like she'd seen her share of challenges and stared them down until they turned tail.

It had been that way for Pauling in the Bureau.

Most of her colleagues had been decent men, but there was always an old-school personality somewhere, sometimes even lurking in someone very young. Attitudes toward women were learned early. It took a lot of life experience to change those beliefs. She almost wished Jardine was here to compare notes.

Her chardonnay arrived and Pauling sipped, feeling the first effects of the martini. It was like putting on something made of silk. Smooth. Comforting. Luxurious even.

As Pauling watched the fake flames flashing in between the artificial logs, she thought about illusion.

Deception.

And trickery.

Yes, Chief Jardine had been satisfied with Pauling's assessment in the morgue.

Which was fine, Pauling thought.

Even though it had been complete bullshit.

CHAPTER TWENTY-TWO

S *ica?*
        Sica was dead.
        Tallon stared at his screen. It made no sense.
Figueroa was dead, too. Who was sending emails from his account? And why?

Tallon needed to get his blood pumping and clear his head from the long car trip and from sitting too long. It dulled the senses.

He needed to clear the cobwebs.

He unpacked, found his swimming trunks and went down to the hotel swimming pool where he swam laps for forty-five minutes, until the water was practically worked into a froth. He toweled off, went into the hotel's small fitness center and pumped iron until the moisture from the pool had evaporated and was replaced with sweat.

Back in his room, he showered and threw on a pair of athletic shorts and a T-shirt and sat down in front of his computer.

During his workout, he'd let the situation marinate in his

mind. He had formulated and tossed aside several different plans of action, until he'd settled on what he was about to do.

Tallon opened his laptop and connected to the hotel's Wi-Fi and sent three emails, pounding them out on his keyboard like machine gun fire.

The first went to the pathologist who performed Figueroa's autopsy, requesting a copy of his report. He fudged a little, implying he'd been hired by the family to look into the matter. Not true. But not totally untrue, either.

The second was to a friend of his who ran a sideline business hacking into other people's computers. He forwarded the email he'd just sent to the pathologist, and asked his friend if the answer was negative, could he get the report for him anyway.

The third email was to Figueroa.

Or, more accurately, to whomever was using his email account.

He kept it short and simple.

You're not Figueroa. Who are you?

CHAPTER TWENTY-THREE

When her eyes began to half-close with fatigue, Pauling signed out of her tab and left the bar area. She passed through a small dining area set up to take advantage of the view of the harbor.

Nautical themes were everywhere, with paintings of old clippers and even a wall tapestry made with fish nets and an anchor.

Pauling skipped the elevator and used the thickly carpeted steps. The hotel was only three stories and she climbed the stairs easily, thinking about her plan for the next day. She had a lot to do, and wanted to get an early start.

Down the hallway, she passed a hotel employee probably doing turn-down services. A couple of the rooms had used room service trays sitting outside, holding water glasses and silver dish covers, usually with a used napkin placed on top and discarded condiment jars.

Pauling got to her room, used her key card and opened the door.

A girl was sitting on the edge of the bed. She jumped to

her feet and Pauling instinctively reached for her gun, but realized she wasn't carrying one.

"No, it's ok!" the girl said. "I just need your help."

She was young, her eyes were wild with fear.

Pauling stepped into the room, but held the door open, and glanced around the entryway into the rest of her room. The bathroom was empty as was the rest of the space.

The two of them were alone.

Pauling crossed quickly to her bag and made sure her gun was still there.

It was.

"Who are you and how did you get into my room?" Pauling kept her voice steady. But she hated surprises.

"My name is Maria," the girl said.

Pauling guessed she was in her late teens. Skinny, with big expressive eyes. Clearly Hispanic heritage, with dark black hair pulled back into a tight ponytail. She had on jeans and a sweatshirt.

"My cousin works here as a maid," the girl said. She sat back on the edge of the bed. Her hands were in her lap and she was wringing the life out of them. "You used to be the police, right? Now you help people?"

"How do you know anything about me?" Pauling asked.

She shrugged her shoulders. "It's a small town. Is it true? Do you help people?"

Pauling was tempted to lie.

"My brother is missing," the girl said. "I can't go to the police."

"I know the police here," Pauling said. "They're very good. I can't help you or do any better than they're doing."

"That's not what I've heard about you," the girl persisted. "You worked for the FBI, right?"

"Jesus," Pauling said. "This town isn't *that* small. How do you know all this and exactly why can't you go to the police?"

"My brother was in Seattle," the girl said, ignoring Pauling's direct questions. "Whoever took him or killed him did it in Seattle. The local cops here won't do anything. They'd be like little people in that big city. Or they'd end up like that guy they found out on the road. By the woods."

The young woman had a way of talking that told Pauling she wasn't a native English speaker. An odd cadence. She also had a thin, sallow appearance. Either a drug user, or malnourished for a different reason.

Pauling was still considering her comment about the dead man out by the woods, when the girl reached into her pocket.

Pauling had her gun in hand and the girl nearly screamed.

"No, it's okay," she said. From her pocket she withdrew a photo.

"Here. Here's a picture of him. My brother."

The girl handed her a small photo, worn but still in good condition. Pauling took it and looked.

There were two men.

The man on the right must have been the girl's brother. Not only because he looked like her, but Pauling knew the man on the left.

Michael Tallon.

CHAPTER TWENTY-FOUR

Sleep refused to grant Tallon's request. It hovered on the edge of his periphery but remained firmly out of his grasp and left him staring at the ceiling, thinking about Figueroa and the mysterious emails.

When his phone buzzed on the nightstand next to him, he was relieved. Tallon glanced at the screen, smiled and answered.

"Lauren Pauling," he said. "I was just thinking about you." And then he added. "I'm in bed."

"What a coincidence," she responded. "I'm in bed, too. And *I'm* thinking about *you*."

Tallon didn't believe her, but he liked her answer.

"Really?" he said, recognizing that it wasn't standard operating procedure for Pauling to flirt. She tended to be a little more direct.

Tallon could picture her, and the sound of her voice always made him happy. Or at least, made him feel better. It was that kind of great voice possessed by jazz singers who frequently light up.

"Yes," Pauling said. "What's new with you since our last case?"

He chuckled softly. That was an understatement. Their last case had been a doozy.

"Working," he said. "You?"

"Same. In fact, I just spoke with a young woman who said her brother is missing," Pauling said. "And when she showed me a photo of him, you were there, too."

Tallon sat up, swung his feet around to the floor.

"You're kidding me," he said. "Was her name Figueroa?"

"Yes," Tallon said, and he heard the surprise in her voice. "Maria. You know her?"

"No, but I knew her brother well."

"Knew?"

He sighed.

"He died last week. Cancer."

"I'm sorry."

"The weird thing is, their family told me that Figueroa's sister was missing," Tallon explained. "And that he had come out here to Seattle to find her."

"Wait a minute. You're here? In Seattle?" Pauling asked.

"Yeah," he said. And then it dawned on him. "You are too?"

"Sort of. I'm on Whidbey Island," she said.

"Business or pleasure?"

"Unpleasurable business."

"Having to do with this girl?"

"No," Pauling said. "Completely separate. Maria somehow found out I was here, my background, and surprised me with a visit. I honestly don't know what to think. And it's awfully strange that you're involved."

"Do you have a way to contact her?" Tallon asked. He was already up and getting dressed.

"Yeah, a cell phone. Are you going to call her?"

"Tomorrow. But right now I've got something else to do."

"Like what?"

"Like, drive to Whidbey Island."

CHAPTER TWENTY-FIVE

After Maria left her room, leaving only a cell phone number and virtually no other information, Pauling got a few hours sleep.

She was up early, not feeling rested at all, but still managed to hit the hotel gym and put in a good workout. Afterward, she showered, dressed and grabbed a cup of coffee from the hotel coffee bar.

In her rental car, she drove out of Pine Beach, along a lonely road virtually devoid of traffic. The staggeringly tall pines towered over her on either side of the strip of asphalt, occasionally parting to reveal distant mountains tinged with layers of deep blue.

As she drove, Pauling thought about the original phone call she'd received, the one back in New York. How it had alerted her to the discovery of the body and the Jack Reacher ID.

Who had that been?

Chief Jardine certainly hadn't called her. She hadn't even known who the hell Jack Reacher was, let alone Lauren Pauling.

Maria Figueroa hadn't called her. If she had, why would she have bothered with the anonymity if she was planning on surprising her in a hotel room a couple days later?

She was in Pine Beach, people had clearly noticed her presence, yet no one had stepped forward taking responsibility for the phone call.

So who had it been?

The coffee was strong and delicious, just the way she liked it. The road crested in front of her and she topped out, saw a long ribbon of highway ahead of her. It was the kind of road she imagined Jack Reacher loved.

She could picture him, putting one foot in front of the other. Nowhere to go. No one to see. Just endless space and possibility.

Pauling thought about what she'd told Jardine.

It's him.

She'd said it with a conviction that she didn't feel. There was no real way to know, of course. Yes, the body was right. The scars were wrong, though. Not correct, and not in the right place.

And they appeared to be recent.

Pauling had said what she needed to say, because to suggest otherwise would lead to more questions. If she'd said she didn't think it was Jack Reacher, then what? It would lead to more questions and require more of her time tied up in bureaucracy.

If it wasn't Reacher, that meant someone had gone to some fairly drastic measures to deceive the police.

Why?

Who would do it?

And the first person who came to Pauling's mind was the obvious one.

Jack Reacher.

Maybe he'd wanted to fake his own death for some reason.

She couldn't come up with a logical motivation, but one never knew. It would be easy enough. Plant his own ATM card on some big lug that looked like him, and disappear forever.

Except, Reacher had already sort of disappeared.

Why would he feel the need to go to this extreme?

What Pauling needed was time. Which is why she lied to Jardine.

By asserting to Jardine that the body was Reacher, it gave her the freedom to investigate on her own.

Starting with the crime scene.

She'd seen the report in Jardine's office, and knew that the shooting had taken place near mile marker 34 on the same rural road she was now on. It was a no-brainer. As soon as she saw the information in Jardine's office, it was a foregone conclusion. Of course she would look at the crime scene.

Pauling drove on, the only car on the road, and after nearly an hour she started to question her method. But as soon as she doubted herself, the crime scene tape came into view, and Pauling pulled her rental car to the side of the road.

She shut it off, pocketed the keys, and looked around.

There was a man.

With a gun.

CHAPTER TWENTY-SIX

Tallon arrived on Whidbey Island in the early morning hours. He crossed the bridge at Deception Pass and studied the terrain. He'd spent a lot of time in mountains both in the United States and abroad. What struck him about this area was the lushness of the foliage. The Pacific Northwest was a place of impressive beauty and Tallon was able to set aside the reasons for his trip to the area and take a moment to appreciate his surroundings.

But only a moment.

His first call was to Maria who stated she couldn't talk and asked to meet at an address she texted him.

His next call was to Pauling, but the call went to voicemail.

Tallon filled his SUV at a gas station with a huge plaza attached. He went inside, bought a coffee and a breakfast sandwich that was piping hot and as soggy as a used beach towel.

Tallon ate and considered his options.

He checked his phone for any response from either

Figueroa's pathologist or his hacker friend, but no one had reached out.

Tallon wadded up his breakfast sandwich wrapper and tossed it into the garbage can nearby.

He had put the address into his phone for the location of the rendezvous with Maria and he would have to be there soon.

It gave him an unsettled feeling.

Figueroa gone.

The strange appearance of his sister in Pauling's room. And perhaps most of all, the appearance of Pauling in the same area, working a separate case.

The confluence of actions made him glad that he had driven to Seattle, as opposed to flying. There were things in his vehicle he would need before he met with the girl.

Now, he drained the rest of his coffee, got into the SUV and drove it around back, behind a semi truck that blocked any view of his actions. The huge truck also blocked any of the security cameras he'd spotted at the back of the station.

Tallon went into the back of his SUV, unlocked the compartment beneath the false bottom and lifted the lid.

Tallon studied the guns. He'd brought a 9mm semiautomatic pistol, as well as a military shotgun outfitted with a pistol grip and plenty of ammo for both. He also had two tactical knives and a Kevlar vest.

He left everything in its place except for the 9mm handgun, which he fitted into a holster concealed beneath his untucked shirt. He closed the compartment and locked it.

Tallon got back behind the wheel and headed out to meet Maria. The location wasn't far away, and in less than a half hour he was pulling into the address at the end of his navigation route.

It was a store at the end of a deserted street. It was a sad combination of retail down on its luck, with a lot of abandoned residential homes.

Depressed was the only word that could describe the locale.

Maria had told Tallon he should drive to the back of the building matching the address she'd provided. It looked like a convenience store, but the windows were painted black and the door was shut. It had security bars across its front.

To the right of the store was an empty parking lot.

Tallon took it all in, and then followed the directions Maria had given him. He drove past the store where a second parking lot, also empty, sat. At the rear of the property was a thin patch of grass with a dead tree and a picnic table.

The picnic table was occupied.

By a young woman.

Alone.

Tallon parked the SUV and approached her.

"Maria?" he said.

She turned and Tallon knew immediately she wasn't Figueroa's sister. She looked nothing like him, and he immediately recognized the presence of drug addiction. The young woman was thin, with dark circles under her eyes and the glassy-eyed look of someone not in her right mind.

The young woman smiled at him and he saw her eyes lift slightly over and to the right of his shoulder.

He turned.

A group of four men had emerged from the back of the building. They were all dressed in similar fashion. Baggy pants, black T-shirts and tattoos covering most of their exposed skin.

Gangbangers, through and through.

One was carrying a baseball bat. Another had a section of lead pipe.

And one had a knife.

Tallon studied their tattoos.

He'd seen quite a few in his time and these were the type he'd seen once before.

In Mexico.

Which meant one thing.

Sica.

CHAPTER TWENTY-SEVEN

"Can I help you?" the man with the gun asked Pauling. His uniform told her he was Pine Beach PD. His baby face told her he was probably new to the force, a young patrolman assigned to keep an eye on the crime scene until further investigation could be conducted. He looked bored.

"Not really, but thank you," Pauling said. She gazed up at the steep bluff to the left of the road.

"May I see some ID, ma'am?" he asked.

Pauling nearly rolled her eyes, but she handed him her driver's license. He was pasty, with a buzz cut and a uniform that looked too small for him. Or maybe he'd gained weight recently and hadn't had time to buy a new one.

"This is a crime scene," the young patrolman said as he handed her back the license. His voice and chest were both puffed up.

"Really? What happened?" Pauling asked.

He shook his head.

"Probably be best if you moved along," he answered. "Nothing to see here, anyway."

Pauling spotted the nameplate above his left breast pocket.

Shepard.

"So I assume the shot came from up there?" she asked, and pointed toward the bluff. To the right of the road, the embankment fell away as it curved slightly upward.

"I can't comment on that, ma'am," he said. He seemed to realize that she knew more than she should. It occurred to him with a realization that arrived in slow motion. "Are you the one that identified the body?" he asked. His pasty skin turned a little pink.

Pauling smiled.

"Yes, I did."

"Chief Jardine mentioned you," he said. Now his voice had a little edge to it. "But she didn't say you were going to stick around and...do whatever it is you're doing."

He finished the sentence awkwardly, and shuffled his feet to work out his discomfort.

"Yeah, I didn't mention that," Pauling said. "Just curious is all."

"Uh huh," he said, his voice less than convinced.

"There a way up there?" she asked him.

He frowned. Clearly, she wasn't paying heed to his suggestion that she move along. But Pauling also saw the conflict.

"I actually just came out for some exercise, wanted to find a good hiking trail," she said. "Is there one back there? I'd like to check out the view."

It was a good compromise. He could help her out, without breaking any kind of rule that would get him in trouble.

"There's a parking area about a quarter mile up to the left. From there, you can pick the eastern trail and it winds up there," he said. "Don't go where there's yellow tape, though. Otherwise, I'll have to come up there."

"No problem, Shepard," Pauling said. "Thanks and I'll see you around."

She got back into her car and drove ahead.

As soon as she was around the bend, Shepard took out his personal cell phone and dialed a private number.

"She's here. Now would be a good time to grab her," he said.

CHAPTER TWENTY-EIGHT

There's always a leader.

An alpha male, surrounded by subservient betas.

Usually the tallest one.

But he isn't always the guy who's going to go first. Sometimes it's the opposite.

The smallest, weakest member of the pack usually has the most to prove and the eagerness to go along with it.

Tallon immediately spotted the leader. Not the tallest, but clearly the strongest, with broad shoulders bulging out of a wife beater shirt, a flat face and dull eyes. No fear, but also no eagerness. He was all business.

The unacknowledged leader was in the middle, and at opposite ends were the weakest of the group. Two of them already several full steps ahead of the pair in the middle.

Unlike the guy in the middle, their eyes were alive with excitement. Bloodthirsty and also tinged with the need to perform. This was perfect for them. Four on one. A surefire victory.

They were anxious to get started, demonstrate their worth by beating a lone man, clearly outnumbered, and demonstrate their value to the group. It was like a home game against a clearly overmatched opponent.

To lose was to bring shame to everyone involved.

Tallon considered drawing his gun and shooting them, but he figured they were armed, to a certain extent, beyond the baseball bat and the lead pipe. He didn't want to be the first one to start shooting. They clearly felt they could handle the situation without resorting to guns as well.

A tactical mistake, but perfectly understandable.

Tallon was more than happy to keep guns out of the equation for now. Mainly because he wanted information.

So he let them come, and turned his back on the girl for the moment. He figured she wouldn't do anything just yet. It wouldn't surprise him if she had a little pistol. Maybe a tiny .25 semi-automatic in her purse. Nothing to be concerned about at the moment. She certainly wouldn't shoot first and guns like that were notoriously inaccurate. The odds of her hitting him were extremely low.

So Tallon waited, knowing that the low men on the totem pole would act first.

And they did.

The two on the ends darted in. One went high and the other went low.

In theory, a decent approach.

An inexperienced fighter might be temporarily frozen with indecision. Do you duck or jump? They were counting on him to do just that, which would provide the perfect opportunity for them to take a baseball bat to his shins and a lead pipe to the temple.

Game over.

Unfortunately for them, Tallon took a third option.

He lunged forward, rendering both of their swings ineffective. To swing a bat and connect with a target required distance. Once inside the bat's arc, power was greatly diminished.

Tallon grabbed the handle of the baseball bat with his left hand, and drove an elbow into the face of the guy with the lead pipe. He felt or heard the man's nose squash beneath the blow.

Tallon continued his momentum, pulling the baseball batter forward and he spread his left leg out, tripping his assailant, forcing him to the ground.

The man's grip on the bat loosened and Tallon wrenched it from his hands and drove the butt of the bat into his temple. Much better use of a club to drive it forward on a straight path. Just as much power with a higher degree of accuracy and effectiveness. The man with the broken nose was still conscious so Tallon utilized the bat again, this time with so much force that he actually felt the man's skull give way. Experience told him that it was probably a blow from which the man would not survive.

Tallon turned and the leader, along with the last of the group, had suddenly realized their odds had shifted quite dramatically.

Any pretense of a quick and savage beating was gone. The man next to the leader glanced at his superior, as if he was asking what he should do.

Tallon knew that any hesitation was deadly in a fight like this.

The leader of the group was already going for his gun.

However, it's one thing to pull a gun when you've got all the time in the world. Maybe when you're showing off for a friend, or practicing in front of the bedroom mirror.

It's an entirely different matter when there's another human being less than twenty feet away who's doing the same.

Tallon was smooth and confident and his 9mm was out

and firing while the leader of the group had barely managed to get a big shiny semiautomatic out of his baggy pants. It was probably a great weapon to wave around at a party when you're full of malt liquor and bragging about how you're going to kill rival gang members, not so great when you're trying to extricate it from your sagging blue jeans when a man directly across from you is beating you to the draw.

Tallon's shots shredded the leader's chest, painting the man's wife beater shirt with blossoming flowers of red blood.

The second man's gun was nearly coming on line when Tallon's bullets hit him in the chest and throat. He got off one shot as he was falling backward, a bullet harmlessly flying directly toward the sky.

For a brief moment, Tallon didn't move as he watched the two gang members complete their fall to the ground. His gun remained in his hand, but he knew they were both dead.

Tallon glanced down at the first two of his assailants and they were completely inert, too.

He turned, expecting to see the girl with either a gun or knife, coming at him.

But he was wrong.

The girl was gone.

CHAPTER TWENTY-NINE

The parking lot was little more than a clearing in the grass that ran about four car widths across.

At some point, someone had thrown in a few bags worth of loose gravel to prevent the grass and weeds from reclaiming their territory. It hadn't worked. There was a lot of green overtaking the gravel. Before long, nature would win.

The lot was empty, and Pauling pulled her rental car into the middle of the space. She got out, locked up, and wished she'd brought some bug spray.

The air was damp and the sun wouldn't be able to cut through the dense pine trees. A perfect environment for mosquitoes and biting flies.

Pauling spotted two trailheads, one to the north, the other slightly back toward the direction she'd just come. That would be the one the shooter had used.

She paused, thinking it through.

Had the shooter parked here, as well? Seen the lone man on the road? He then would have driven past him, hurried into position and taken the shot. A simple sequence, most likely accurate. But not the only plausible scenario. Pauling needed more information.

She considered the setting.

It was definitely a remote location. Traffic virtually nonexistent. No one to see the murder. Hearing it would be a different matter. Sound carried well in the mountains due to the thinner air.

Pauling wondered if Chief Jardine had been thorough in canvasing the area to check if anyone had seen a car parked in this spot around the time of the murder. There were no residential areas nearby. Tough to knock on doors when there weren't any houses. But had someone heard the shot? Pauling made a note to check on whether or not there were any active hunting seasons. If not, a gunshot would certainly catch someone's attention.

She wondered how long the man had been walking on the road. Had he come from Pine Beach? If so, that was at least two hours walking on the road. Surely someone would have passed him.

And a man with a physique similar to Reacher's would not go unnoticed.

Pauling made a mental note to see if Jardine had posted any descriptions of the man in the morgue. 6' 5" with massive shoulders and arms corded with muscle. Walking. Alone.

Someone must have seen him.

Pauling realized she was avoiding going into the woods so she walked ahead, took the trail and was soon climbing vertically on a path covered mostly with pine needles and loose stones.

Along the way, she kept her eye out for anything that didn't fit, but she had little hope. It rained here every day, practically. If the shooter had left behind any evidence, the chances were slim it had still survived intact.

The nature of the kill was interesting, too. Downhill shots

were always a little tricky and the more she climbed, the more convinced she was there was more investigating to do. Her initial assessment of Chief Jardine was one of competence, but perhaps lacking in experience. Pauling could help with that.

She climbed and the trail twisted left, toward the road. Pauling soon discovered the site.

There was an enlarged area cordoned off with yellow crime scene tape. The pine needles were scattered and what grass had managed to grow in the space was heavily trampled.

No doubt the shooter had retrieved the shell casing, or casings. She assumed it had been one round fired. A head shot that had clearly gotten the job done. But she made a mental note to follow up with Jardine.

Pauling studied the ground.

Had the shooter been standing? Or had he gotten down on the ground, in a true sniper position to take the shot?

No way to know now, Pauling thought, as she studied the highly contaminated crime scene. There was clear evidence that someone, most likely Jardine and her officers, had trampled all over the site. The grass was matted down and the dirt underneath was slick and muddy.

Where the trail widened it created a ledge that wasn't big enough to be called an overlook, but would have provided enough room for a single shooter to get comfortable. It was less than a quarter mile from the parking area, so the killer would have needed to be fairly confident no one would be coming along the trail.

Concealment would also have been possible, to a certain extent.

The shooter hears someone coming along the trail, slides off the edge of the embankment and he's not visible from the trail.

That is, if he heard someone coming.

Pauling glanced down, over the ledge.

Maybe some disturbance visible, maybe not. Impossible to tell and even if someone had been there, how would she know if it'd been the cops or the shooter? She didn't have a personal crime lab to analyze fibers.

She looked down the line of sight to the road.

By her estimation, Pauling put the distance at roughly eight hundred yards. Not an exceedingly difficult distance for a good rifleman, but not a cakewalk, either.

Downhill.

Wind shear from the bluff could be unpredictable.

The distance said less about the shooter's ability, and more about his confidence.

When he set up here, he had no problem with the length of the shot or the gusting winds that swirled enough to affect the trajectory of a bullet.

A breeze picked up speed behind her and pine boughs above her swayed in a delayed reaction. Pauling realized that not a single car had passed since she'd been occupying the vantage point.

With nothing else to analyze, Pauling turned and headed back toward her car. She watched as she walked, looking for anything discarded or missed by the Pine Beach PD, but she found nothing. Either they'd collected everything, or there'd been nothing left by the perp, which was Pauling's guess.

Back at the clearing, she walked toward her rental car as she heard the sound of a vehicle approaching.

Surprised, she glanced up as a black SUV slowed.

The windows were tinted.

Pauling had her door open, and watched the SUV.

It had slowed even more.

And now, it stopped.

CHAPTER THIRTY

S he was satisfied, in every sense.

Over the course of a week she had made a clean kill on a tricky downhill shot, assassinated a senator, and fulfilled her every sexual desire to the fullest extent possible.

It had been a successful sequence of events for the shooter known to her employers and fellow mercenaries as Grace.

The name was an inside joke.

Not her real name, of course.

She'd chosen it for the multiple meanings. Grace under pressure. To grace someone with her presence. But mostly, hoping her victims prayed for grace before drawing their last breath.

Now, she watched as the gates to Sica's compound opened, and she drove forward, to the main house.

When she parked and got out, she felt the eyes of Sica's bodyguards on her. Grace could read their minds.

This was the assassin?

A petite, red-haired woman who barely weighed a hundred pounds soaking wet?

But then they saw her face, the lack of fear, the utter lack of emotion and she could see their appraisals instantly shift.

Grace was shown inside to a study that smelled vaguely of marijuana and whiskey. Sica stood before a floor-to-ceiling window that looked out on a wide expanse of green grass, patrolled by two men with machine guns.

Sica turned to look at her and his face was partially obscured from view by the slight haze of smoke. There was no surprise registered on his face. Grace knew that Sica had done his homework. He also most likely knew it was very dangerous to meet in person. Not for her.

For him.

If things ever went sideways, anyone who saw her face would become a marked man.

A bodyguard stepped into the room and took up a space next to the door.

That was okay.

Grace wasn't here to take out Sica. No need at this point, not with another fat paycheck that was most assuredly on its way to her.

Besides, this was the wrong place and the wrong time.

If it came to that.

If that moment ever did arrive, though, it would be relatively easy despite the little man's paranoia. Paranoia without intelligence amounts to ineffective busywork.

Grace watched the little Mexican drug boss and waited. He pulled a cigar from his shirt pocket and offered it to her.

She shook her head.

"You don't smoke?" Sica asked.

"I'll get enough secondhand, thank you."

He took a long drag on his cigar and blew the smoke upward.

Grace waited.

Sica smiled at her.

"You like movies?" he asked. "Big Hollywood...what do they call them? Blockbusters?"

Grace didn't bother to respond.

"I do," Sica continued. "And when I see a good one, I'm happy. You know why? Because I know there's going to be a sequel. Always. There is always a sequel. I know, I know," he said, holding up a tiny little hand. "Usually they're not as good. But still, I enjoy them. That's what we have here. A sequel."

Grace nodded. She knew that was why she was here. There was a huge payday to come, all she had to do was hope this little man got to the point. And soon.

"Part one of your job was completed to everyone's satisfaction," Sica said. "However, the next step that was to be completed by others, did not get done. I need you to do it."

Sica produced a sheet of paper, folded into a small square. He handed it to Grace.

"A word of advice?" Sica said. "You seem like a very confident woman. That is good. I sent four confident men to complete Phase 2. None of them came back."

Grace's face remained impassive.

"That was a bad sequel," Sica said. "Like Jaws 2. I think you will do very well with the third in the series. Like the Indiana Jones movies? Remember? First one was great. Second one not so good. Third one excellent. And the fourth was a disaster, but there won't be a fourth in our little adventure, will there?"

Grace replied simply. "No."

"Let me show you something," he said. Sica walked past her and she followed, through the foyer to a side door that led down to a large subterranean room with an open square in the middle.

Sica walked up to the edge and pointed down. Grace glanced into the pit, saw the alligators at the bottom.

If he was trying to intimidate her, it didn't work. She'd already heard about Sica's little pet collection.

"I call them my evidence processors," he said. "Better than a deep grave. My enemies become alligator shit." He laughed, a high-pitched little giggle.

"One more thing," he said. Sica led her back upstairs to a bedroom. He opened the door and Grace saw a young woman chained to a bed. The young woman's face was a mask, her eyes blurry and unfocused. Heavily sedated.

There was something familiar about the face, and Grace instantly knew who the girl was.

"She's the sister of one of the men who murdered my brother and his daughter in Mexico," Sica said. "I'm using her as bait. Once you complete your part of the job, she'll go for a swim. Do you know what I mean?"

Grace nodded. She knew exactly what he meant, because she had worked with Nathan Figueroa once, a long time ago.

This would be the part where he threatened her, Grace thought. Imply that if she didn't fulfill her part of the deal, she too would end up in the pit.

But he displayed a little more intelligence than she had given him credit for and he implied the threat rather than directly stating it.

It didn't matter, she thought, as she walked out of Sica's compound.

She allowed a small smile to appear on her face.

Grace had known all along that Sica's phase 2 plan wouldn't work.

Because she knew Michael Tallon personally.

Oh, yes.

She knew Michael Tallon very, very well.

CHAPTER THIRTY-ONE

Pauling watched as the black SUV with tinted windows came to a stop. She had the door of her rental car open, and her hand slipped inside her jacket to the butt of her gun.

The SUV idled for a moment, and then pulled away.

Pauling debated about following, but decided against it. She had arranged to meet with Tallon at Pine Beach.

She got into her rental car, fired it up, and made her way back from the direction she'd come.

Once in town, she parked and spotted Tallon outside the restaurant where she'd suggested they meet.

"Made-from-scratch biscuits," he said, pointing at the sign in the window.

She laughed. "Men always think of food first," Pauling said. They hugged and Tallon's body felt warm and hard. As always, she felt the flash of physical attraction to him. He wasn't what you would call a handsome, leading-man type, but he was attractive in a rugged kind of way.

They went inside and Pauling ordered scrambled egg whites with a biscuit and honey on the side.

Tallon chose coffee and a biscuit.

After some small talk and catching up, Tallon said, "So tell me how you ended up out here."

Pauling filled him in on the mysterious phone call saying Reacher was dead, and then the story about a dead body believed to be Jack Reacher. Pauling knew that Tallon wondered why she had gotten a plane so quickly to come out and investigate, but he didn't bring it up.

"So you have your doubts that it's actually him?" he asked.

"I'm not convinced," she said. "In fact, I'm fairly certain it isn't him. I just haven't shared that with the local police yet, but eventually I will. I just wanted some freedom of movement for the time being."

"And you still don't know who called you about it?"

"No."

"Well, someone wanted you out here," he said. "It stands to reason it's the same party responsible for the murder, right?"

"Most likely," she said.

"Who else?" Tallon asked. "It's not like the local police would place some mysterious call asking for help. First of all, they wouldn't ask for help, and if they absolutely had to, they wouldn't hide it. Too much red tape these days."

The waitress brought their biscuits and placed them on the table and topped off their coffee.

"A certain level of sophistication is on display here," Pauling said, taking a forkful of egg white. It was bland. She added some salt and pepper.

"Yeah," Tallon said. "You don't manufacture a fake ATM card very easily. Unless they stole it."

"From Jack Reacher?" Pauling asked, raising an eyebrow. "I don't think so."

Tallon cut a section of biscuit off with his fork. Chewed.

"Damn, these are good," he said. "I should have ordered two."

"The sophistication angle is an interesting one," Pauling said.

"Sure," Tallon agreed. "I mean, forget the ATM card. How the hell did they know about your history with Reacher? Didn't all that happen in New York?"

"It did."

He stabbed another chunk of biscuit with his fork. "Do you have any enemies in this part of the country? Someone who would want to lure you out here with a jacked-up story about Reacher? No pun intended."

Pauling took a sip of coffee.

"Not that I know of. I've got a sister in Portland, but she's a civilian. Nothing to do with me or my background.

"What about you?" she asked.

Tallon told her about Figueroa, his missing sister, and the gangbangers.

"So you don't think the woman who was in my hotel room is actually his sister?"

"No," Tallon said. They had already mutually described the woman and arrived at the conclusion that the woman in Pauling's hotel room had been the same woman on the picnic table who'd orchestrated the ambush.

"So if she wasn't Figueroa's sister, who is she?" Pauling asked.

"Great question," Tallon said.

Pauling ran through some scenarios in her mind, none of them making much sense. Something nagged at her and suddenly it occurred to her.

"If they knew about my history with Reacher, they probably know about my history with you," she said. "Or, put another way, they know about *your* history with *me*."

They both watched each other as the implications reached home.

"What if the goal wasn't to lure me out here?" Pauling asked. "What if the point was to lure *you*?"

Tallon's phone buzzed and he looked at the screen.

"Shit," he said.

"Problem?"

"Maybe part of the solution," he said. "It's the pathology report on my friend Nate Figueroa," he said. Pauling watched as he scrolled through a message on his phone.

"Any surprises?" Pauling asked.

"Yeah, you could say that."

He signaled for the check from the waitress.

"Nate Figueroa didn't die of cancer," Tallon said.

The waitress placed the check on the table and Tallon threw down a twenty.

"He was poisoned."

CHAPTER THIRTY-TWO

Zurich, Switzerland

Gregory stood before Gunnella Bohm and struggled to maintain eye contact. Partly because he knew she wasn't happy. And partly because she was nearly six inches taller.

"Is this about our friend in Seattle?" Bohm asked him. Of course, she already knew the answer to the question. She just wanted him to know that nothing he could say would come as a surprise.

"Yes," Gregory said. "It appears that one of the Department members has been doing some extensive freelance work."

"Freelance work is their livelihood, Gregory," she countered, just to see what he would say.

"True, however certain projects require preapproval, of which she did not obtain."

Bohm raised an eyebrow.

"Grace has always been fiercely independent," she said. "One of the things I admire about her."

Gregory cleared his throat. "Independence in contractors can become a liability, which I believe is now the case."

Bohm turned her back on him and studied his reflection in the window. He didn't move. She knew he wouldn't.

"Your next step?" she asked him.

"The best way to handle an issue in the Department, is to let the Department take care of it themselves," Gregory said. "Under my direction, of course."

"Is that a logical assumption?"

"I believe it is," Gregory answered.

She turned and faced him.

"The Collective is not something that does things on hunches and whims. Our actions are direct, concrete, and therefore consistently effective. Only those who demonstrate those same abilities have a place here."

"My course of action will have the result needed with maximum efficiency."

Bohm smiled at him.

"Who in the Department are you going to utilize?" Bohm asked.

"Moss."

Bohm nodded. It was who she would have chosen if she'd been in the same position. Of course, she would never have allowed herself to be in this position in the first place. Gregory hadn't directly errored, but sometimes errors of omission were the worst kind.

"Timetable?" Bohm asked.

"Immediate."

"Collateral damage?"

"None."

Bohm didn't believe that, and she suspected Gregory didn't believe it, either. But it was the right answer.

"Deliver your next update twenty-four hours from now," she said.

The door beyond slid open, triggered by the remote control in her pocket.

Gregory turned to leave.

"One last thing, Gregory," Bohm said.

He glanced back at her.

"The Department must come out of this situation stronger, not weaker. Any negative effects on The Department will greatly disappoint me."

He nodded and left.

Bohm slid the door shut and picked up her phone.

CHAPTER THIRTY-THREE

Pauling and Tallon left the café.

He was going to check into the same hotel as Pauling and they would join forces.

It only made sense.

They parted on the sidewalk. Pauling walked along the street and while her biscuit had been good, she knew she would have to spend a little extra time on the treadmill during her next workout.

Maybe she and Tallon would work out together.

She smiled at the thought. What *kind* of workout that might be, who knew?

Pauling allowed herself the thought of how nice a romantic rendezvous with Tallon would be. She found him very attractive and unless her radar was completely off, she sensed that the feeling was reciprocal. Hell, he'd flirted with her on more than one occasion.

As she walked, she glanced in the display windows of stores along the street. Mostly nautical knickknacks and tourist stuff. A local art gallery. A used bookstore. A brewpub proudly featuring craft brews of the Pacific Northwest. Maybe she would try that later.

A little physical affection would be nice, she thought, as her mind returned to Tallon and their shared hotel.

It had been awhile since her last relationship, with an investment banker who spent most of his time on his yacht, sailing the world.

She'd spent a week with him in the Mediterranean, stopping at ports for good food, great wine and beautiful scenery.

Eventually, though, she'd gotten bored with both the trip and the banker. Plus, when she suggested they take things more casually he had responded by proposing to her. A curious reaction and the opposite of what she had just requested.

So that had ended, and there really hadn't been anyone since.

Now, she checked her phone as she walked to her rental car. There were several messages from friends back in New York, along with some case updates in her email.

She would have plenty of catching up to do when she got home. Maybe she would grind through her email back at the hotel so when this was all done she wouldn't face a mountain of unresolved issues back in New York.

Pauling unlocked the rental car and slipped inside. She fired up the engine and was about to put it in gear when a cloth was slapped over her face and an arm reached from the back, clamping across her upper body.

She struggled, dropped her phone, and tried to reach her gun.

But her vision blurred and then she saw nothing.

CHAPTER THIRTY-FOUR

The first to arrive was the only American in the Department. His name was Moss, and as he strolled through the Seattle airport, he looked like a man on a casual business trip. Tan jeans, a T-shirt beneath a light-weight sport coat, with a briefcase and single strolling suitcase.

He looked neither young, nor old. Short, brown hair that may or may not have had a touch of silver.

While his age wasn't apparent, his physical condition certainly was.

Lean, but powerful. A former athlete, maybe, who'd never stopped competing.

Moss was unhurried, but walked with a purposeful stride. The kind of guy who always arrived at least ten minutes early to a meeting.

The single suitcase was all he really needed, because he knew the Collective had shipped everything he needed ahead of time. The car was already parked short-term, and when he stowed his suitcase, he was satisfied to see two bags already in place.

The Collective was highly efficient.

Having an unlimited budget didn't hurt, he knew.

As always, though, it came down to intelligence. The more information the better. And the right kind of information.

Moss left the airport, headed toward Whidbey Island.

He'd never gone after another member of the Department.

It was highly unusual and carried with it a great deal of risk. However, the folks back in Zurich had doubled his normal fee. He failed to mention to them that he knew his target, personally.

He smiled.

Moss would have been happy to kill the bitch for free.

CHAPTER THIRTY-FIVE

Tallon sipped from a small black coffee and wondered where Pauling was.

He'd dumped his gear at the hotel, and ducked around the corner for some caffeine. The carbs from the biscuit had made him feel a little sluggish.

Now, he logged onto the café's Wi-Fi and checked his phone.

Nothing.

It was a little strange.

They had just talked a few hours ago, and agreed to meet at the hotel. He thought for sure she would either be working out or, more likely, just working. He knew that Pauling's company was very successful and high-end. He was sure running a business like that placed a lot of demands on her time and attention. Still, it was unusual for her not to communicate.

Tallon wondered where she might have gone.

A man and a woman walked into the coffee shop, vehemently discussing what sounded like a pending real estate offer. Something about a condo and whether or not a chandelier was included. It seemed like, according to the woman, if the chandelier wasn't included then the deal was off.

Tallon watched the street, waiting.

He considered his options and how long he was willing to wait.

When his phone rang, he saw the blocked number.

"Tallon," he said.

"I'm with Lauren Pauling," a woman's voice said. "Join us in an hour at the address I'm about to text you."

The call disconnected and then beeped with the incoming text message.

Tallon clicked on it and it automatically opened his map app. The address was forty-five minutes away, near Deception Pass, but in a remote location, far from any town.

He left the café, retrieved some items from his room and soon had the SUV pointed toward the address he'd been sent.

Tallon knew that voice.

He couldn't quite place it.

But it was someone he knew.

As he drove, he tried not to concentrate on it too much.

He hoped it would come to him.

And soon.

CHAPTER THIRTY-SIX

Pauling came to and quickly realized two things. One, her arm was numb because it was handcuffed to an iron pipe.

And two, her ass hurt.

She was sitting on a cement floor and from the musty smell, she assumed it was a basement.

There was no one around.

Her cell phone was gone. Her head hurt, but she knew it was from the chloroform and not because she'd taken any blows to the head.

It was important to stay positive.

She wasn't scared. She'd been taken hostage once before, but that was totally different because Jack Reacher was involved.

Now, she didn't have Reacher to rely on.

A door opened above her and two people descended, pushing a third in front of them.

Both of them were small.

One man.

One woman.

In front of them, was a girl.

Pauling instantly knew it was Figueroa's real sister, not the imposter who'd no doubt been working for the man in front of her.

The woman was small, but wiry. With bright red hair and pale skin. Her eyes passed over Pauling and registered nothing.

The other person was a tiny man with dark skin and jet black hair. Mexican, if she had to guess.

Two heavyset men descended the staircase and used a set of handcuffs to chain the girl next to Pauling.

"This is her?" the Mexican said, pointing at Pauling. "She's old!"

"Screw you, pal," Pauling said.

The little Mexican walked toward her and kicked her in the stomach. She saw it coming and managed to twist enough to block some of the kick.

"You trying to hurt me with those size 5s?" she asked.

A small smile tugged at the red-haired woman's mouth and then it was gone. She glanced over at the little Mexican man who looked like he was going to try to kick Pauling again.

"So much bait," the man laughed. "I'm glad you agreed to doing it here. I think it's for the best. Still, all this for one man. Overkill, no?"

The red-haired woman didn't answer.

The little Mexican man walked over to an opening in the floor and looked down and then he looked at Pauling.

"They're going to love a taste of you," he said. "After my men have had their fill."

"Whatever, oompa loompa," Pauling said. The same little smiled showed briefly on the red-haired woman's face.

The Mexican looked confused. "Oompa lompa? What is this?"

He looked at the red-haired woman who didn't answer.

"Google it, asshole," Pauling said.

They pair left then, climbed the stairs and Pauling heard the click and lock of the door.

She turned to the young woman beside her.

The girl was unconscious. Pauling wished she could lift her hand and check her pulse, but it was impossible.

"Hey, it's okay," she said.

The girl didn't respond.

Pauling struggled to maintain her breathing, admitting the kick hurt a lot more than she let on.

The little man had said the bait was all for one man.

She knew what he meant.

And wondered what Michael Tallon was doing.

CHAPTER THIRTY-SEVEN

There was a time for planning.

And a time for action.

Tallon believed strongly that the moment called for less planning and more action.

Of course, instinct told him what he was going to find. Pauling had already figured out the situation. She had started to uncover it when they were at the café.

While it was true Pauling had been lured out here, it wasn't the end game. They had used her as insurance to get Tallon in their crosshairs.

And he thought he knew why.

The thing that tied it all together was Figueroa.

And Sica.

Not Alberto Sica. Because he was dead. Gunned down by Tallon, Figueroa, and the rest of their crew.

Unfortunately, they'd killed Alberto Sica's daughter, too. Firefights have a way of getting out of control.

That one had been no exception.

There had long been rumors that Sica had family who'd fled to the United States. Tallon was now sure that they were the ones behind this. They had somehow managed to poison Nate Figueroa, and figured it would be easier to kill Tallon by luring him into their territory.

Now they had Pauling.

And probably Maria Figueroa.

Tallon knew what was in the compound he now faced. A gate. Multiple bodyguards. Sica himself. And probably a hired killer or two. Maybe even the same one who'd shot the Reacher lookalike.

No, the time for planning was over.

The next step would be a direct approach.

Literally.

His SUV was reinforced with a crash bar at the front, as well as a rear guard. But the crash bar in front was connected to the entire frame of the vehicle. With a full tank, it was a heavy vehicle.

And he put the big vehicle in high gear, four-wheel drive, and pressed the accelerator to the floor. The road leading up to the gate was slightly downhill and it helped him reach nearly eighty miles per hour before he hit the gate straight on.

No airbag deployed because he'd removed it during the vehicle's customization. The gate was blasted off its hinges and one of the sections screeched down the side of Tallon's SUV as he plowed through it and straight toward the front door of the compound's main building.

He continued straight ahead, the SUV pulling hard to the left because either there was something pinned to the vehicle or because the frame itself was knocked out of kilter.

It didn't matter because the engine was powerful enough to drive straight up onto the front porch and barrel right into the front door.

Not surprisingly, the door didn't hold and the SUV was in

the middle of the building's main room where gunfire erupted.

Tallon flung his door open and rolled from the truck immediately after the front door gave and the SUV skidded to a stop, its engine smoking and transmission grinding to a halt.

He rolled away from the vehicle as it shuddered on, and he came up with his gun in hand.

The first targets were easy.

Mexican gangbangers, Sica's men, no doubt. They were not trained to be attacked and they were in the process of directing their fire toward the vehicle.

They sprayed it down with hundreds of bullets.

Complete overkill.

Only one of the men seemed to realize the driver was no longer in the vehicle.

He was the first man Tallon killed.

His own gunfire was lost in the thunderous noise.

After Tallon dropped the first of Sica's men, he took out three more in quick succession. None of them had seen him and their attention was on the vehicle or their weapons as they paused to reload.

When all three dropped, though, attention turned to Tallon.

By then, he had already scrambled to the left of the entrance, taking cover behind a metal bin containing firewood ready to be burned in the fireplace.

Bullets dinged off the metal. Metal shards combined with wood chips rained down on him.

Tallon crawled to his left again and spotted two of Sica's men trying to flank him around the crashed SUV.

He shot both of them, two sets of double taps to the chest.

And suddenly, the cabin was silent.

Tallon ran to his right, around the back of the SUV and came face-to-face with Sica. The little man had a huge machine gun he was trying to bring to bear.

Tallon was much faster.

He knocked the gun down, placed the muzzle of his pistol against Sica's forehead and pulled the trigger.

The little man dropped to the floor and suddenly, Tallon was facing a woman with bright red hair and an arm around Pauling's throat.

She had a gun to Pauling's head.

"Hey," the woman said. "Tallon. Long time no see."

"Nowhere to go Grace," Tallon said.

"We miss you in The Department," she said. "It's not the same without you."

"That was a long time ago," Tallon said. "Besides, it was hard to know who you were working for." He nodded his head. "No amount of money is worth being employed by scum like that."

"Speak for yourself," Grace said.

Tallon looked at Pauling. She returned the gaze with a frank expression. Not scared. Just waiting.

"You going to kill her?" Tallon asked Grace. "And Nate Figueroa's sister, too? Two innocent women? That's what you've become?"

"The girl's downstairs," Grace said. "Alive."

"How magnanimous of you," Tallon replied.

"A contract is a contract, though," Grace answered. "I honor all of my contracts, which includes you, and her."

Tallon saw Grace's finger tighten on the trigger but he knew there was no way he could pull his gun in time.

And then suddenly, he didn't have to.

Because Grace's head exploded in a shower of blood and brain tissue.

Moss stepped out from behind her, holding an automatic

with a silencer attached. Smoke curled from the weapon's muzzle.

Pauling had fallen to the floor alongside Grace, but now she scrambled forward, toward Tallon who lifted her to her feet.

He looked her over.

"Are you okay?" he asked.

"Yeah. Jesus, who was that woman?" she asked, glancing down at what was left of Grace.

"She was bad news."

The man with the gun stepped over the dead body.

"Pauling, this is Moss," Tallon said. "Moss, this is Pauling."

"Can't believe I had to bail you out again," Moss said to Tallon.

"I'm getting Maria," Pauling said.

Tallon looked at Moss.

"They sent you here?" he asked.

Moss nodded.

"Was she your only contract?"

Moss smiled, glanced at the SUV in the middle of the room.

"That was quite the entrance," he said.

CHAPTER THIRTY-EIGHT

Two days after the shootout at the cabin, Tallon and Pauling sat with Moss at the same coffee shop where Tallon had been sitting when he'd gotten the message from Grace that she had Pauling.

"Doctors say Maria's going to be okay," Pauling said, and put her phone away. "It didn't look like they'd gotten to her yet."

Tallon nodded. "Her father is flying out this morning to bring her back to Minnesota. He's very glad she's okay, considering what happened to Nate."

Moss shook his head. "Nate was a good guy." He paused. "Zurich gave me the background information, if you want to hear it," Moss said.

"Who's Zurich?" Pauling asked

"Probably better if you don't know," Tallon said. "A small group of people over in Europe who run The Department, which is what we called ourselves. At least, when I was still in it." He glanced at Moss. "You guys still call yourselves that?"

Moss shrugged. "Unofficially."

"So tell us," Pauling said.

"The operation to take out Alberto Sica was a success, but they also killed his daughter."

Moss paused, giving Tallon the opportunity to chime in.

He stayed silent.

"Alberto's brother, Archibald, was here, in Seattle. When he found out about his brother and niece, he hired Grace to kill a Reacher lookalike and send word to Pauling. They figured by bringing her out here, they could lure you in."

"So who was the guy they killed?"

"A bare knuckle brawler known to some folks in the underground. So when word was sent out looking for people who matched Reacher's description, his name came up."

"So I'm guessing when the people in Europe found out Grace was freelancing, that's when they sent for you," Pauling said to Moss.

"Grace was off the reservation. Had been going that way for a long time, apparently. She shot the senator because apparently he was threatening to expose one of the people in Europe. That person then hired Grace, who not only took on the job of the senator, but also Sica's highly lucrative contract. Same general area. Two birds with one shot, kind of thing."

"So they found out they had two people off the reservation. Grace, and someone on the inside," Tallon said.

"That's when Zurich sent me in," Moss said. "They already knew where Grace was. So they sent me the coordinates. That's how I got there about the same time you did."

"How did people in Zurich know?" Pauling asked.

Tallon glanced at Moss, then back at Pauling. "They know everything. Their resources are unmatched."

Moss glanced at his watch. "Speaking of resources," he said. "I've got a plane to catch."

He stuck out his hand to Pauling and then to Tallon. "Any time you want to come back to The Department, we can always use the help," he said.

Tallon held up his hands.

"I'm retired," he said.

Moss laughed and left.

Pauling looked at Tallon.

"Department of what?" she asked.

Tallon shrugged his shoulders. "Murder."

He drained the rest of his coffee.

"Now what?" Pauling said.

"My room is paid through tomorrow," he said with a grin. "Why don't we put it to good use?"

Pauling smiled, finished her coffee.

"Took you long enough to ask."

CHAPTER THIRTY-NINE

Z URICH, SWITZERLAND

The body had been in the chilly waters of Lake Zurich for at least twenty-four hours before a visiting investment banker in a water taxi spotted it floating a hundred yards from shore.

A call was made and the police arrived. They promptly loaded the body onto their boat where it was decided there was no need to call a medical examiner to the scene because the cause of death was obvious.

Two bullet holes in the center of the dead man's forehead told the story.

From her perch high above Lake Zurich in the Collective's conference room, Gunnella Bohm watched the police boat motor away with the body of her former colleague.

Gregory had made several mistakes.

The fact was, his first lapse in judgment had already

earned him a death sentence, the errors that followed simply provided additional support, albeit that evidence was completely unnecessary.

Once the decision to remove an individual from the Collective had been made, there was no going back.

Gunnella Bohm was well aware of Gregory's impending fate long before she officially ordered his removal from the Collective. It was both an instinctive sense that the man was not going to last, as well as a decision based on fact. Every member of the Collective was under various levels of surveillance, depending upon their experience, risk level and Bohm's ongoing assessment.

Gregory had been a holdover from her father's regime. A mistake that she never would have made.

The sins of the father, she thought.

Now, the sun was setting and the police boat was out of sight. The sky above the water took on the color of amber as the arrival of another crisp evening took shape over Lake Zurich.

Gunnella Bohm stepped back and pressed a nearly invisible button recessed along the edge of the large window. A white metal screen silently rolled down from above and covered the window, leaving the conference room as black as night.

By then, Gunnella Bohm was already gone.

ABOUT THE AUTHOR

Dan Ames is a USA TODAY Bestselling Author and winner of the Independent Book Award for Crime Fiction.

www.authordanames.com
dan@authordanames.com

ALSO BY DAN AMES

STANDALONE THRILLERS:

THE RECRUITER
KILLING THE RAT
HEAD SHOT
THE BUTCHER

BOX SETS:

AMES TO KILL
GROSSE POINTE PULP
GROSSE POINTE PULP 2
TOTAL SARCASM
WALLACE MACK THRILLER COLLECTION

SHORT STORIES:

THE GARBAGE COLLECTOR
BULLET RIVER
SCHOOL GIRL
HANGING CURVE
SCALE OF JUSTICE